TAKE MY BREATH AWAY

During the 50th anniversary remake of *Cleopatra*, movie star Patty Carter's ex-husband Jason is found dead in his trailer with a knife in his chest. No one seems to be safe as the murderer strikes again and again. Whilst fighting off suspicions that she is the killer, Patty is torn between handsome insurance investigator Tony Marcus and equally handsome actor Matt Archer. But Patty is keeping back a secret about Jason, and Tony is determined to discover the truth, even if he is falling desperately in love with her . . .

SALLY QUILFORD

$\blacklozenge$

TAKE MY BREATH AWAY

Complete and Unabridged

LINFORD
Leicester

First published in Great Britain in 2013

First Linford Edition
published 2014

A catalogue record for this book is available
from the British Library.

ISBN 978–1–4448–2011–9

Published by
F. A. Thorpe (Publishing)
Anstey, Leicestershire

Set by Words & Graphics Ltd.
Anstey, Leicestershire
Printed and bound in Great Britain by
T. J. International Ltd., Padstow, Cornwall

This book is printed on acid-free paper

1

'No, no, no, no,' Director George Cassius boomed from behind the cameras. 'You are carrying the Queen of Egypt, not a sack of coal. Cut!'

Patty Carter, playing Cleopatra, rolled out of the rug and rubbed her elbows and hips. She looked towards the open studio doors, where sunshine flooded through. Far in the distance, near the studio gates, she could see the protestors with their slogans. It was a group complaining about caucasian actors playing ethnic roles. Patty had given an interview on breakfast television only the day before. 'If white actors could only play white characters, it would also mean there could never be a black Romeo or Juliet. We're actors and we act out roles. Those roles don't have to be constrained by our own ethnicity. It also means that Elizabeth Taylor, a Jew, could not have played Cleopatra either, and that would be a sad loss to the world.'

So much for being on location, thought Patty, shivering. Nowadays no one went to Rome, or anywhere else for that matter. Ancient Rome and Egypt would be put into the film using computer graphics.

'Sorry, Patty,' said Andy Paxton, the actor playing Appolodorus. 'I lost my footing.'

'It's okay, Andy.' Patty grimaced. 'The floor broke my fall.'

Jason Carter, playing Julius Caesar, stepped forward and helped her up. 'Come on, old girl,' he said in the deep Welsh tones that had made him every bit as famous as his fellow countryman, Richard Burton.

'Oy, less of the 'old girl'. I am still twenty-five years younger than you are.'

A make-up girl stepped forward and dusted Patty's nose. It had been really hot and sweaty in that rug. Perspiration ran in rivulets down her back.

'Thanks, Olivia,' Patty said with a smile.

George Cassius had come out from

the darkness to join them. 'We'll try that again, shall we? And this time, put the rug down with a bit more finesse and not as if you're working for some substandard removal firm.'

'Give us a moment, Cassius,' said Jason. 'We've done this scene fifty times already. How many takes do you need of Cleopatra being rolled out of a rug?'

'Excuse me?' said Cassius, turning on Jason. 'Is your name down on this film as director? No, it isn't. I realise you've done a bit of directing, Carter. Who can forget your last film, which was basically *Die Hard* on a train? The one where the vicar saves the day?' Cassius snorted with laughter. 'I expect a bit more of my actors than hanging on to a train by wires.'

Jason muttered something under his breath and turned away.

Patty saw a faint sheen of sweat on his brow, leaving tracks in the heavy stage make-up. 'Jason needs to rest,' she said quietly.

'I'm fine,' said Jason, turning on her

with an angry expression.

'I know you are. But it wouldn't hurt any of us to take a break.' She turned to Cassius and talked firmly. 'I'll walk with Jason to his trailer. I want to discuss something with him.'

'Am I the director here or am I not?' Cassius turned to one of the runners. 'Carla, go and fetch me a coffee whilst I try and take back control of my film.'

'It's Carmen,' said Patty, smiling encouragement at the terrified girl. 'Come along, Jason. We need to talk.'

By that time, Jason was trembling violently. 'You mean he needs a drink,' said Cassius disgustedly. 'If you need a rest, Carter, I'll give you a rest. A good long rest! Please, don't rush back on my account.' Cassius muttered something about washed-up old actors.

'He is not washed up,' said Patty. 'He is one of the best British actors alive today, and you know damn well that this film wouldn't work without him.' She would have said more, but Jason looked seriously ill.

Five minutes later, Patty sat next to him on the sofa in his trailer. He was still perspiring, but the trembling had abated.

'I'm sorry I was angry with you,' he said. 'You are my favourite ex-wife, no matter what I might say when I'm taken ill.'

'I know,' Patty said with a smile. She became serious. 'Jason, you have to tell them. Cassius's schedule is gruelling enough for a fit person, let alone . . . '

'No. You know what Hollywood is like, Patty, especially when it comes to underwriting films like this. Any sign of weakness and they won't entertain an actor.'

'So you'd rather them think you are an alcoholic. Is that it?'

'It's not a bad thing to be known as a hell-raiser. It makes you seem interesting. As long as you turn up to set on time.'

'Jason, you're fifty-five years old. Being known as a hell-raiser at your age is beginning to look a bit pathetic.'

'Did I say you were my favourite ex-wife? I meant second favourite. Maybe even third.'

'Oh yes, I'm sure Miss Centrefold nineteen-ninety-three was your real favourite.'

'She had a good mind, that girl, no matter what you say.'

'Did she really?' Patty raised a sardonic eyebrow. 'Come on, we'd better get back to work.'

'Is it my imagination, or is Cassius worse than the last time we worked with him?'

'Much worse,' said Patty. 'But this is his last chance, isn't it? I hear that if he doesn't succeed in this remake, he's out of the game. He's brought too many studios close to bankruptcy with his mad ideas. Then there was that actor who was killed on his *Ben Hur* remake a couple of years ago. He pushes people too hard and takes too many risks. Yet for all that, he's a genius.'

'I do fear for our lives sometimes,' said Jason.

'We survived him before. We'll

survive him again.'

'Our marriage didn't survive last time.'

'Hmm, but that had more to do with Miss Centrefold and me being pregnant.'

Jason looked forlorn. 'I'm sorry, Patty. About all that.'

'I know you are.'

'But you still won't take me back?'

'No, Jason. You're one of my best friends. Just leave it at that, shall we?'

'I'm an idiot.'

'Oh yes,' Patty laughed. 'You are.'

She left him in his trailer and was taken by the assistant, Carmen, to wardrobe and make-up to get ready to re-do the scene, only to find that Cassius had moved on to something different. Two very large men in security uniforms were waiting in the wardrobe department.

'We're filming the scene where Marc Antony sees Cleopatra for the first time,' said Barbara, the wardrobe mistress and main dress designer. She was a middle-aged woman, thin as a rake, with wild purple hair and terrible dress sense. On that day she appeared to be wearing a sack dress that matched her hair. She was also an Oscar winner, so was clearly much better at dressing others.

Patty was used to scenes being filmed out of sequence, but she had expected to get all her personal scenes with Jason completed first, because he had another film to go on to the following week.

'But that's a huge procession,' she said to Barbara. 'I thought we weren't filming that till next week.'

'What Cassius wants, Cassius gets,' said Barbara. 'He's bringing in all the extras, so we've got to work like mad to get them all ready.'

'I'd better let you sort me out then,' said Patty. 'So you can get on.'

'You're a nice woman, for an actress,' said Barbara. 'Most would be screaming from the rooftops by now.'

'I got all that out of my system in my second big film,' Patty said. 'And I wasn't even the star. In fact I think I died in the first five minutes, but boy did I think I was a star.'

Barbara laughed and helped Patty into a gold outfit, including a dress and a headdress that weighed more than Patty did. 'There's real gold in the stitching,' Barbara explained. 'And the jewels in the headdress are real, hence those two security men waiting to escort you to the set. Cassius insisted on everything being authentic.'

Patty stepped into the dress and then waited patiently whilst Olivia did her make-up, which was even more elaborate than she wore in the earlier scene. It was thick, hot and sticky, and she thought it made her look a bit clown-like, but it would look wonderful on film.

The two security men practically had to carry Patty to the set. By the time they reached it, she was bathed in perspiration again, and Olivia had to re-touch her make-up again as the thick dark eyeliner threatened to run down Patty's cheeks. She was then surrounded by assistants making sure her dress looked right when she sat up on the huge golden carriage.

As before, everything was done in front of a blue screen, but it still took ages to set up. Patty sat up on a large carriage that only looked as if it was being moved by slaves. It was actually on a rolling road, giving the illusion of motion. When the film went into editing, a computer-generated image of ancient Rome would be added in. About fifty extras surrounded Patty, including the actors playing slaves who were 'carrying' the carriage, and those playing Romans watching the procession. Their numbers would be increased in the editing process to make it look like tens of thousands had attended the procession. Only eagle-eyed viewers would notice that everyone in the crowd was repeated hundreds of times over in the background.

It was a process that Patty found interesting, but soulless. She rather wished that like Elizabeth Taylor in the original film, she was surrounded by thousands of real people. It would make it easier to act as if she were really in Rome and really a living goddess. That might also be easier if they had been shooting the scene outside.

As Jason was absent, despite the fact that he was supposed to also be in the scene, they filmed around his role, concentrating instead on the reaction of Marc Antony to Cleopatra.

Marc Antony was played by an up-and-coming young actor called Matt Archer. He had made his name in a television fantasy drama called *The Last Gladiator*. Marc Antony was his first big role. He was very handsome and already had his own following of ardent female fans. He stood at the far end of the set, so that the camera could get his reaction to the scene in one take. The supporting cast, including the actress playing Caesar's wife, Calpurnia, sat around him, trying to keep cool whenever they were not being filmed.

'No, no, no,' said Cassius, cutting the scene again. 'Marc Antony, you are seeing the most beautiful woman who ever lived. You're not looking at the menu in a burger restaurant.'

'Pity, because I'm starving,' said Matt. 'I know you don't allow your actresses to eat, George, but surely you could allow some food on set for the rest of us.'

Patty suppressed a smile. She was pretty hungry herself and could have murdered a plate of chips.

'We'll start again,' said Cassius. 'Remember the story. Cleopatra is riding into Rome to see her lover, Caesar, and to show her devotion to him and to Rome, and then . . . Wait a minute . . . ' He put up his hand. 'What the hell is going on over there? Are you dealing drugs?'

Some of the extras were huddled together in a group. Cassius stormed onto the set and swept the group apart. 'What the . . . ?' He snatched something from one of the extra's hands, and said, 'Is that a Cornetto?'

'It's blooming hot in here,' said the extra. 'So I thought I'd sell a few to cool us down. I got the idea off Wikipedia. Some bloke in the original Cleopatra film sold gelato to the extras.'

'Ooh, can I have one?' said Patty, giggling.

Matt walked across the set, took an ice cream from the Italian extra's hand and then held it up to Patty theatrically. 'A gift for a living goddess,' he said, showing his even, white teeth in a dazzling smile.

Before Patty could get hold of it, Cassius had snatched it from Matt's hand. 'If you get one drop of ice cream on that dress, I will kill you both,' he said. 'Look, what's this? Strawberry sauce?' He rubbed at Patty's dress, and she looked down to see a red stain on the bodice of her dress. 'Wardrobe! Wardrobe! Come and sort out this mess immediately! What is wrong with everyone today? I am trying to make a film here. A film that will make everyone realise how much they've underestimated me. Everyone seems intent on ruining my vision. Why do I give any of you the chance to work with me? I am a genius and you lot, you are nothing. Carla, come here.'

Carmen stepped up onto the set. 'Go and fetch His Lordship, and tell him that he is needed on set. Now!'

'His Lordship?'

'Jason Carter, you idiot!' Cassius took a deep breath. 'We'll film him receiving Cleopatra on the steps. I hope he hasn't had too much to drink.'

Patty was about to say something, but clamped her lips shut. Instead she allowed herself to be helped down from the carriage by the security guards. Now came the hard bit: walking across the set to where Caesar and the Roman dignitaries would be waiting. She practised it once or twice, whilst waiting for Jason to arrive. It was hard going, and she could not wait to get rid of the heavy outfit and into something more comfortable. Surely, she thought, Cleopatra did not suffer this much to look beautiful. She had a vague idea that the massive spectacle shown in films about the queen would have been much lower key in real life. Like the time she went to see the changing of the guard at Buckingham Palace as a child and realised that they were just a bunch of soldiers swapping shifts, albeit in a very grand way.

As she practised walking, she became aware of a commotion at the studio door. Carmen had returned and was sobbing loudly. Without thinking, Patty threw off her headdress, sure that Jason had been ill again. Only she would know how to deal with him, because he was so adamant no one else could know.

She still found it hard going even wearing just the dress, and was only vaguely aware of the security guards shouting after her as she half ran, half stumbled to the studio door and out into the lot where the trailers were parked.

'Jason . . . ' she called, as she headed for his trailer. It was the biggest one there, as befit the star of a major film. 'Jason, I'm coming.'

She climbed the steps and hurtled

through the door, her elaborate outfit getting stuck in the process. Forgetting to take care with it, she pulled it free and staggered into the trailer. 'Jason, love . . . ' She stopped mid-sentence, and the sweat that trickled down her back became icy cold.

Jason Carter was sprawled back on the sofa with a knife sticking out of his chest.

2

Andy Paxton watched the early morning television. 'I look good, carrying that coffin, don't I?' he said to his wife. The news once again returned to the funeral of film megastar, Jason Carter, which had taken place the day before. Several famous actors and directors were called upon to give their views on his death. All spoke about his professionalism and his love of life, and the fantastic body of work he had left. The camera panned to Patty Carter — pale, drawn but still utterly beautiful — standing at the graveside with her young son. Then it panned to a buxom blonde, who was said to have been a famous centrefold, and clearly the victim of unscrupulous plastic surgeons who did not tell her when to stop.

Cindy Paxton bustled around getting their twin sons ready for school. She was Andy's third wife, and twenty years younger than him. She had been working as a waitress when they met, and Andy was a customer in the restaurant. She knew him from the teen soap, but she would not admit it. Instead she had feigned disinterest, which had only made him more interested. There was the issue of his second wife, but Cindy became pregnant as quickly as possible. As Andy had not wanted bad publicity at a crucial time in his career — the prison sentence in his twenties had been bad enough — he had no choice but to divorce his wife — paying her a lot of money in the process — and marry Cindy.

'Honestly, Andy, the poor man has died,' she said, but her voice lacked real conviction. Andy knew she was only saying it for the sake of their sons. She was a good mother in that way.

'I know, and I'm sorry he's dead. I didn't know him well, but he seemed okay in those few scenes we had together. But this footage is going out all over the world, Cindy. I'm there, carrying his coffin with three world-famous actors. Me, Andy Paxton: the dad on a lousy teen soap. I told you getting into a George Cassius film would help me. And you said he made rubbish films.'

'He does make rubbish films. All that sex and violence.' Cindy lowered her voice. 'And all that silence. Can't he afford a scriptwriter or something?'

'You're missing the point, babe,' said Andy. 'Ken has had tons of calls.' Ken was Andy's agent. 'I'm being invited to all sorts of shows to talk about this murder. Including some in America. Ken has set me up for some screen tests whilst I'm there. I thought things would be slow till the film came out, but this murder has put the spotlight on everyone.'

He picked Cindy up and spun her around. 'We're made for life, babe! We'll move to Beverley Hills, yeah? Or Malibu. We can have a house on the beach.'

'I like the sound of that,' said Cindy, quickly getting over any sympathy she might have felt for Jason Carter.

'Yeah, I hate to say it, but Jason Carter getting murdered is probably the best thing that ever happened to us.'

'Shh,' said Cindy. 'Not in front of the twins.'

'The way of the world, babe,' said Andy. 'When one door closes, another one opens.'

'Or you could just open the door, because doors work like that,' said Cindy.

'Huh?'

'I dunno. It's something I read on Facebook. I think it means you can do things for yourself instead of waiting, or something.'

'Stuff that! I'd rather have people opening doors for me, babe, and there'll be a lot of that now. You just wait. You'll be the wife of a mega-star.'

Andy kissed Cindy and the twins and left for the studio. He was late, but he did not care. He was a big star now. He must be, to be asked to carry Jason Carter's coffin. It was George Cassius's idea, and whilst Jason Carter's family had refused at first, Andy had managed to convince them of his sincerity. He was good at that. 'That's what they call good acting, babe,' he had told Cindy at the time.

Okay, so those other actors who were pallbearers had looked down on him, but what did he care about a couple of Oscar winners?

He drove to the studio, imagining what his life would be now. He could see it all. Cindy in diamonds, and the twins in the best gear. He would have to find a way to get Natalie to America without Cindy knowing, but he was an old pro when it came to juggling two women. Odd, though, that all Jason Carter's exes talked about him as if he were a god, yet Andy felt sure his own exes spent their spare time sticking pins into voodoo dolls of him. He had a brief notion that maybe he should have treated them better, but he pushed that thought aside. If they had been better wives he would not have had to look elsewhere for love and affection.

The traffic was lousy. He would have a word with Cassius about that. A man of his standing should not have to drive himself to the studio.

He was getting out of his car when he saw the group of protesters near to the studio entrance. The ones who did not think a white south Londoner should be playing an Egyptian. 'Damn,' he thought. He would have a word with Cassius about that too. He should not have to put up with all that rubbish.

One of the extras broke away and started to walk towards him. It was a tall, lean man, with a hard face and, as Andy remembered, even harder knuckles. His stomach knotted. There was someone else in the crowd that he recognised too, but they stayed where they were. 'Hiya, Vince,' he said warily to the man who approached him. 'I didn't have you down as an activist.'

'Just admiring the scenery,' said

Vince. 'That Patty Carter is a beaut, isn't she? A real lady too. She spoke to the protestors all nice-like. Got them eating out of her hand, she has. Yep, a man could lose his head over a woman like that.'

'What really brings you here?' Andy looked around for the media. There had been a lot around since filming resumed, and he did not want to be photographed talking to the Vince Astwells of this world.

'We miss you, Andy. Down at the club.'

'I don't do all that anymore, Vince.'

'What does that Eagles song say, Andy? You know, that one about checking out but never leaving. Yeah, well that's what the guv said about you. You've had a break and you've deserved it, but it's time to get back in the game. Especially now you're going to be such a big star. The guv sees a whole new world opening up for him.'

'I told you, I don't do that anymore. Don't forget I took a fall for the guv. I did five years for it.'

'Yeah, he's really grateful about that. Why else would a girl like Natalie be spending time with you?'

'What?' Andy's mouth became dry. He had a flask of whisky in his pocket, which he sorely needed; but his hands, which were curled in fists, would not budge from his sides.

'She's a gift from the guv, to thank you for all your support in the past. Mind you, I bet . . . what's her name? Cindy? I bet she wouldn't be too pleased about it if she knew.'

'Look,' said Andy, with as much dignity as he could muster. 'I may be a cheating husband and I might have been a crook at one point. But now I'm straight, and I'm staying that way. So you tell the guv to . . . ' Andy stopped as he saw a group of people with cameras approaching. 'Tell him I said goodbye.'

Andy all but fled to the studio, his heart hammering. He had left that life behind and had no intention of going back to it. He was a waster, even by his own estimation, but his days of pushing drugs were gone. At the time he had been in the grip of a devastating habit, and he had not thought of the consequences of his actions. Then one of his clients, a young prostitute, had died, and he had been brought face-to-face with himself. He still did not like himself all that much and he still had his vices. But they were not the sort of vices that could lead to some-one's death.

He barely heard George Cassius screaming at him for being late. The morning passed in a haze. Once or twice, during the breaks, Patty Carter asked if he was okay. Vince was right about her. She had a way of making people feel important.

'Yeah, just a bit shocked still by what happened to Jason,' he lied. In truth, he was more worried about his own life spiralling out of control. Earlier that morning he thought he had the whole world at his feet. Now that world had turned on its axis, taking him back in time to a place he no longer wished to be.

'Paxton,' said Cassius. 'We're doing your death scene again.'

'We've done it,' said Andy.

'It was rubbish. Besides, the reel got damaged. So we're doing it again. Come on.'

Later everyone said it was Andy Paxton's best performance — that of a man willing to die for what he believed in and for the queen he had loved forever. It was only as he was speaking the lines about his feelings for Cleopatra that he realised he really did love Cindy. He had been a fool over Natalie, but he would make it up to his wife and sons. He drank down the poison, grimacing slightly at the brackish taste of the water. Everyone thought that was a realistic part of the performance too.

Then Andy Paxton dropped dead on the set.

3

Tony Marcus knocked on the door of the chief detective's office. Around him the police station bustled with activity. He could see a picture of Jason Carter up on a board, along with another picture of a man who had been virtually unknown, until his death thrust him into the limelight.

'Come in.'

He opened the door to see Sam Brady sitting behind the desk, snowed under with paperwork. Sam was a good-looking man in his late thirties.

'Tony! Come on in.' Sam held out his hand. 'How long has it been?'

'Too long.'

'Can I get you a coffee?' When Tony nodded, Sam went to a small table which held a coffee machine and poured them both a cup. 'So how is life for you out in California, spying on errant husbands

27

and wives?' Sam gestured to a seat, which Tony took gratefully. He sat back down in his own seat and took a sip of his black coffee.

'Not bad,' said Tony, grimacing. 'I'm here about something a bit more important than that. I'm representing the insurers of the film, *Cleopatra Rises*. You know of Cassell and Keep?'

'I've heard of them. They're insurance investigators, aren't they?'

Tony nodded. 'That's right. I work for them now, and we're investigating the claim for Jason Carter's death.'

'The man was murdered, Tony. He didn't kill himself, if that's what you're thinking. There's been another death since.'

'I know, but we have to cross all the 'T's and dot all the 'I's. I just wondered what you could tell me about the people involved.'

'Have you been to the set?'

'No, not yet. I hear Cassius is insisting on finishing the production, despite the setbacks.'

'The man is a lunatic,' said Sam.

'Is he a suspect?'

'Everyone is a suspect. It is noticeable that Jason Carter had shot most of his scenes, and that Cassius is now using archive footage to fill in the rest. So none of us would put it past Cassius to have stabbed Carter to garner promotion for his film. He's in a lot of trouble financially, and this is his last chance with Hollywood. He takes too many chances with the safety of actors and extras, and his ideas are far too extravagant, yet the results aren't always that wonderful. They say that when he's good, he's brilliant, but that when he's bad, he's capable of creating more turkeys than Norfolk in the weeks coming up to Christmas. Did you ever see his remake of *Ben Hur*?'

'I watched it before I came to Britain, to get an idea of the man. It's pretty dire to say how much controversy it caused.'

'Yes, it also led to the death of an actor. Despite that, Cassius would not halt filming. It took a law suit from the actor's family to stop him from using the footage of the death. He said it was more realistic and tried to argue that the actor had signed off on it when he took the job. Like I said, the man is a lunatic.'

'Who else do you fancy for it? I hear the ex-wife was questioned.'

'That's right. Patty Carter. She's a stunner. Every bit as lovely as Liz Taylor was when she played Cleopatra. They were married when she was eighteen and he was forty-three, and then divorced a year or two later when he was caught *in flagrante* with some centrefold. On the day he was murdered, she had blood on her outfit, and no one knows how it got there. She insists it must have been when she went to see him after he was found, but it was seen by witnesses before then. Cassius thought it was strawberry sauce — something about some extra selling ice creams — but it was definitely human blood. We're running tests on it to ascertain whether it's his. The main problem is that she was in the company of others from when she put that dress on, to when Carter's body was found. There's film to prove it. You know how it is nowadays. They don't just make the film. They film the making of the film for DVD extras. It is possible the blood was on her hands. But she didn't help her case by upping and disappearing after we let her go, pending further questioning. She was gone till the funeral, and refuses to say where.'

'Interesting.' Tony had already seen that in the papers, with the headlines *The Mystery of Patty's Missing Week*. 'What was her relationship with Carter? It seemed odd them working together when they'd divorced.'

'Well that's just it, Tony. They got on very well together from all accounts. She seemed to understand him better than others did. They told everyone they were delighted to be working together again, and as far as we can tell they meant it. Anyway, it's not just Carter now, as you know. There was another murder on set.'

'Yes, the guy playing Apollodorus was poisoned the day after Carter's funeral, wasn't he?'

Sam nodded. 'Cassius had insisted on continuing the filming. He carried on with the less important scenes. One was of Apollodorus taking poison. It's near the end of the story chronologically, but apparently they film scenes all out of order.' Sam grinned. 'I've learned a lot about the film business this last week or so. The actor was only supposed to drink water, but it was poisoned and he died in agony a few hours later. It was . . . ' Sam looked down at his notes and reeled off the name of a poison with at least fourteen syllables. 'Apparently it's something they use in the special effects department.'

'Was there anything to link him to Carter?'

'Not as far as we know. They'd starred in things together before, on television, but they weren't close friends because Paxton was very much a supporting actor and played bit parts, with 'bit' being the operative word, until he got onto that teen soap. They weren't enemies either. You know how the actors talk about each other: 'He was such a professional'. That's what Andy Paxton — the guy playing Apollodorus — said about Carter when he died. And that's what was said about Paxton when he died.'

'Was Patty Carter there at the time? When Paxton died, I mean.'

'Yes, she was, but again she was in full view of everyone and the death scene was done on a different set. She had no chance to touch the water that he drank.'

'Who else had access to the props?'

'Who didn't?' Sam sighed. 'There were hundreds of people moving around at all times — cameramen, extras, props people, wardrobe, special effects, runners, assistant directors, hangers-on, tea ladies, uncle Tom Cobley and all. The same goes for Jason Carter's death. There were no cameras around the trailers. It was something the actors insisted upon, so that they weren't on screen the whole time and could relax properly in that area of the compound. We don't have anything to show who went into his trailer and killed him. Hundreds of people had access to the place.'

'Didn't he have bodyguards?'

'He wasn't that sort of actor. Or rather, he used to be the kind to be chased around by reporters and fans all the time, but he had slowed down a bit. From what I can make of Carter, he was a proper actor. Not just a star, if you know what I mean. Before filming, the paparazzi were more interested in young Matt Archer, the bloke who is playing Marc Antony. He's the latest hot young thing and has been linked to nearly every starlet in Hollywood. There are rumours about him and Patty Carter. Both deny it and give the 'we're just good friends' line.'

'Do you think this Archer might have seen Jason Carter as a rival and finished him off?'

'Could have, but it doesn't make sense. The Carters were divorced. They got on well, but as far as we know, they weren't in love anymore.'

'Do you mind if I snoop around a bit, Sam? I don't want to tread on any toes, but . . . ' Tony paused.

'I imagined you planned to snoop anyway, but it's good of you to ask. If you turn anything up though, you come straight to me. Finding the killer or killers is far more important than whether or not an insurance company has to pay out.'

'Absolutely.'

'Maybe you could help me,' said Sam. 'In the event of his death, who does Jason Carter's insurance payout go to? We know his will leaves everything to his son by Patty Carter.'

'It's the same,' said Tony. 'But the kid is only ten or eleven years old, so I don't think he came along and stabbed his own dad to get rich.'

'No, but she might have.' As Sam spoke, the telephone on his desk buzzed. He picked it up and listened for a few minutes. 'And you can get the warrant?' he asked. 'Good.'

'What?' said Tony, seeing Sam's excited expression.

'The tests on the blood from Patty Carter's dress came back. It's definitely Jason Carter's.'

4

Sam let Tony accompany him to the set. They also took a couple of female police officers. They reached the studio just as Patty was filming the scene where Cleopatra orders her handmaiden to drink poisoned wine.

Patty Carter lounged on a chaise longue, being fanned by two slaves. She wore a sheer dress, the fabric of which, by some clever design, became thicker around her breasts and pelvic area, giving the illusion of nudity, whilst also covering her.

'Drink it,' Patty Carter said, watching as the handmaiden, with trembling hands, put the cup to her own lips. The coldness in Patty's voice and in her eyes made Tony shiver. In that moment he truly believed that this woman would be capable of cold-blooded murder. She showed absolutely no mercy, and no remorse. It also seemed to Tony that the young actress playing the handmaiden was genuinely scared; as well she might be after what happened to Andy Paxton. He hoped that proper checks had been made this time.

The girl was just about to drink when a loud crash from the studio startled everyone. The young actress dropped the golden cup on the floor, spilling the contents.

Patty's face immediately changed to one of concern. 'Are you alright?' she asked the girl, putting her hand on the girl's shoulder. Tony was surprised by how quickly she could change emotions, and he could not help wondering how good an actress she was. Perhaps she really was capable of being heartless one moment and caring the next.

'Cut! What happened?' A voice rang out, and a wild-looking man with frizzled ginger hair moved from behind the cameras. Tony recognised him as George Cassius. 'Who did that?' Judging by his face, Cassius was capable of murder, at least in that moment. 'We'll start again, shall we? Fill it up again!'

'Just one moment,' said Sam Brady. 'Mr Cassius, I'm afraid we're going to have to halt production for now. We wish to speak to Ms Carter.'

'Well you can't. I have a film to make and a schedule to keep. As if things weren't bad enough with people dying all the time.'

'Yes, very inconsiderate of them,' said Tony, ignoring the annoyed look that Sam gave him. He had promised to keep quiet. He looked back at Patty, who was watching him with interest. Their eyes met and he immediately thought about launching a thousand ships. Then he remembered that was Helen of Troy, not Cleopatra. In that moment Patty seemed to him to be Cleopatra, Helen of Troy, Joan of Arc and any number of classical heroines that men did daring deeds for.

She had particularly startling eyes. The dark Egyptian-style kohl surrounding them accentuated their violet depths. A man could drown in eyes like that, and he was not surprised that Jason Carter had once loved her. But what had destroyed that love and sent him into the arms of another woman only months after they were married? Was it possible that Patty Carter was a nightmare to live with? Tony felt suddenly ashamed, as if he were blaming the victim for the wrongdoings of the man who had hurt her.

'What can I help you with, Detective?' she asked, turning her head to Sam. Her voice was low and husky, with a nice timbre that made Tony think of being read soothing bedtime stories.

'Would you come with us to the station please, Ms Carter?' asked Sam. 'We have things we would like to discuss with you in private.'

She looked as if she might argue, but instead she said, 'Very well.'

'Just a minute.' A very handsome young man stepped out from the shadows. Tony looked at him with interest, recognising him as Matt Archer from photographs shown to him by his bosses at Cassell and Keep. 'Don't just go with them like that, Patty,' said Archer protectively. 'You need a lawyer.' *Et tu*, Archer? Tony thought.

'I don't need a lawyer,' she said, laughing incredulously. But there was something in her violet eyes. Fear perhaps. Or guilt?

'Perhaps it's best,' said Tony, immediately wondering why on earth it mattered to him. Yet something about her made him want to protect her. She obviously had Archer for that, though why that should bother him, he did not know.

'We will, of course, allow you to consult a lawyer, Ms Carter,' said Sam Brady through tight lips.

'It's fine,' said Patty. 'I'll come. I hope you'll allow me to change. I'm not exactly dressed for visiting a police station.'

Receiving the affirmative from Sam, Patty Carter, flanked by the two police women and the wardrobe and make up assistants, went to her trailer to change.

41

Meanwhile, George Cassius had a huge tantrum, threatening to sue the British police, the British film industry and the British Queen.

'You promised you wouldn't speak,' Sam muttered to Tony whilst they waited.

'I know. I won't. But I want to listen in on the interview.' He wanted to know all about Patty Carter and why she might murder her ex-husband so many years after their divorce. Already he was coming up with reasons why she could not possibly have done it, but they all came down to the same reasons really: those wonderful eyes that could be so cold one minute and so warm the next. You're pathetic, he told himself. But if he walked away now, it would be like walking out of a film halfway through, and never knowing how it ended. He had to know about her and put to rest the unease he felt when he looked at her lovely face.

'It's beyond your remit now, Tony. You have no jurisdiction here.'

42

'Come on, Sam. I won't be in the room. I can do it through a two-way mirror. For old time's sake. I did help you find that serial killer who fled to America. You had no jurisdiction there, as I remember.'

Sam sucked the air between his teeth. 'You keep out of her sight. Don't give her any reason to call foul on this, Tony. Too many killers get off on technicalities nowadays, claiming we haven't followed procedure.'

'You can trust me.'

'I'm not so sure, where she's concerned. You've gone all dreamy-eyed.' Sam grinned. 'Honestly, you and actresses!'

Tony resented being reminded of that. 'I'll still do the job I've been sent to do.'

An hour later, Tony watched through a two-way mirror as Sam and a female officer questioned Patty Carter. There was a solicitor sitting next to her, but she seemed happy to talk anyway. She had changed into a black roll-neck sweater, with black leggings that showed off her long, lithe legs. Her hair, which had been covered by an elaborate headdress on set, was surprisingly short, framing an elfin face. She wore no make-up and was lovelier for it, though for the first time Tony could see faint dark circles under her eyes. She had clearly had a few sleepless nights lately.

'You understand that you are being interviewed under caution,' said Sam.

'Yes, I understand.'

'Tell me about your relationship with Jason Carter.'

'Jason and I were divorced, but we remained good friends for the sake of our son.'

'Can you elaborate? How did you meet? Fall in love? Divorce?'

'We met on a film. George Cassius directed that too. That man seems to have been there at all the major junctures of our lives. Our meeting, our divorce, and now . . . ' She swallowed hard and looked down. 'Now at Jason's death.' The latter part came out in a whisper.

'Are you saying Cassius did it?'

'What? No. I'm just thinking aloud, I suppose. Jason and I met when we were filming a George Cassius film. Jason was the star, and I had a small role in that. I was eighteen years old and it was the beginning of my career. Then we made a film together, with Cassius, a couple of years later, and the stress of that, amongst other things, led to our divorce. And now . . . well, now this.'

'It wasn't your ex-husband's affair with a centrefold — his third wife? — that led to your divorce then?'

'That was a symptom, not the cause. As odious as Cassius is, they say he is a genius. When he gets it right, he gets it very right. But he loses control and then starts to get it very wrong. The first film Jason and I worked on together with him was the one time he got it right. The second film was when he got it very wrong, and it affected all of us. He's struggled a bit since then I think.'

'Yes, but we're not talking about

Cassius,' said Sam Brady. 'We're talking about Jason Carter. Your ex-husband. You say you remained amicable for the sake of your son, but it must have hurt you deeply when he left you — a beautiful, intelligent woman — for a topless model. You were pregnant at the time too, weren't you?'

Patty smiled, a little sadly. 'Yes, it did hurt dreadfully at the time. Our divorce was very acrimonious, as any number of tabloids from that era will tell you. But then there came a time it didn't hurt anymore. I got over it. It was more than ten years ago after all. Then, as I said, because of our son, we learned to get on, until there came a time when we actually liked each other again. Jason was one of my best friends, and I think I was one of his. Believe me, Detective Brady, if I had wanted to kill Jason, I would have done it ten years ago when I was at my angriest. I wouldn't wait till now to do it.'

'Revenge is a dish best served cold, they say.'

Patty shook her head vigorously. 'If you're mentally unbalanced and can't let go of the past, yes, maybe that's true. But I'm not. I'm very resilient. Also, I learned to understand Jason.'

'You forgave him?'

'I wouldn't say that. If I had forgiven him I would have taken him back, but I could not live with a man who did not respect my place as his wife. But afterwards I accepted him for what he was. I accepted that he had something of a God complex, and that this meant he was easily swayed by people who appeared to worship him, women in particular. Jason thought he was being nice to women if he slept with them. He was doing them a favour by spreading the love around and he wanted them to like him. He was a people-pleaser to an extreme degree. But he forgot that he wasn't pleasing me when he did those things. He never learned either, with any of his wives. It's sad, because I don't think making other people happy ever made him happy. He was a bit sad on that last day . . . '

'About what?'

'I don't know. Probably nothing in particular. He wasn't very well.' She clamped her lips shut, and Tony had the strange idea that although she seemed to have spoken the truth so far, she was suddenly being evasive. 'I think he was worried about getting old and being alone.'

Tony felt sure that was not it.

'So are you saying he might have committed suicide?' asked Sam.

She appeared to think about it for a moment, before shaking her head. 'He wouldn't do that. He wasn't the best of fathers, but he did love our son. He wouldn't leave him in that way. No, someone killed him.'

'How did the blood get on your dress?'

'I honestly have no idea. Jason was definitely alive when I left him and I was not even in that outfit. I went to see Barbara, the wardrobe mistress, and she told me that Cassius had decided on a

48

different scene. I was helped into the dress and headpiece . . . it was really heavy, I can tell you, and from then on I had two security guards with me. But I didn't kill Jason. Just as he would not commit suicide for our son's sake, I would not take my son's father away from him.'

'Yet your son stands to inherit a great deal of money. Your husband was a rich man and if the insurers pay out, the dividend will be enormous.'

'My son does not need that money and neither do I. Jason has always been generous with him, and I am more than capable of making my own living.' She lifted her small chin proudly. Tony had an image of Cleopatra again, regal and dignified.

'Why did you run away after the murder, Ms Carter?' asked Sam Brady. 'It was all very mysterious. Even the paparazzi could not find you.'

'Perhaps you should have asked me that instead of getting your news from the tabloids, Detective Brady. I did not

49

run away.' She spoke emphatically. 'I ran *to* my son. His father had just been murdered, and he needed me to be with him.'

'So why couldn't anyone find you?'

'Because I chose not to be found. I'm not one of those actresses who marches her children out for the press. I keep my home address secret so that my son is not bothered all the time with photographers. So that he can grow up as a normal child.'

'We will need that address, Ms Carter. Can you supply it to us?'

Patty Carter's eyes suggested that Sam had asked too much of her. But she was also an intelligent woman. She must have realised she could not refuse. 'I trust this will remain secret and that it won't be leaked to the press.'

Sam laughed incredulously. 'No one here would leak your address.'

'Are you sure?' She raised a disbelieving eyebrow. 'I've seen the Levinson report.'

'We're not like that in this station and

if anyone did that, I can assure you they would be severely reprimanded.'

'I suppose I'll have to trust you.' Patty gave them an address in Surrey, which Tony filed away in his head for future reference. 'I don't want my son bothered with all this.'

'We may need to pay a visit and make a search of the property.'

'I trust you'll have a warrant,' she said. It was the first time that Tony had seen her really rattled.

'We will arrange that,' said Sam. 'Where is your son now?'

'He should be at school. Later he'll be at home, with his nanny.'

'Perhaps then we can arrange the search during the school hours, so as not to distress him.'

'Yes,' Patty said, breathing a visible sigh of relief. 'Yes, that would be acceptable. Thank you.'

'With a warrant, of course,' said Patty's solicitor, speaking up for the first time.

Sam nodded in agreement. 'We'll

have the warrant.'

'Are you planning to let my client go today, Detective Brady?' asked the solicitor. 'At the moment, you have no real evidence that she killed Mr Carter, apart from a tiny spot of his blood on a dress that not only witnesses, but cameras inside the studios, prove that she was not wearing when she last saw him.'

'I also changed straight out of one outfit and into another,' said Patty. 'In fact, I'm pretty certain the cameras filming the 'making of' programme showed me changing. There was no blood on that outfit, was there?'

'Yes, that is true,' said Sam. 'We checked it and found no blood.'

'So really, you have no reason to keep her,' said the solicitor. 'Either charge my client or let her go, Detective Brady.'

'We will allow Ms Carter to go for now,' said Sam, reluctantly. 'But you must tell us where you are at all times, Ms Carter, and we will be searching your house.'

5

Olivia Cooper put a coin into the vending machine and punched in the alpha-numeric code to receive a can of diet cola. She had something on her mind and needed to go somewhere quiet to think about it.

'Damn, it's warm again,' she muttered as she handled the can. 'The machine is broken,' she said, louder. 'It's not chilling the drinks.' There were people all around but no one really took much notice of her. They were all too busy doing their own thing.

'Just give it a kick,' said Matt Archer, coming up behind her. He put his arms around her waist and nuzzled her neck.

'That won't make the chiller work,' she said, smiling. As fellow Australians who had moved to Hollywood to make it in the movies, Matt and Olivia had a lot in common. Of all the pretty girls on

53

the film, he seemed to like her best. At least when Patty Carter was not around. Every woman paled in significance when Patty was in the room, and Olivia could not blame Matt for being bewitched.

She opened the can and took a swig of warm, treacly liquid, grimacing as she did so. There was a table full of food next to the vending machine, so she put it down on that and snuggled into Matt's very hunky embrace.

'What's wrong?' asked Matt, turning her to face him. 'You looked troubled when I was walking over.'

'Oh, just something I have to work out. When something like this happens . . . you know, first Jason Carter's death, and then Andy Paxton, you start to imagine you've seen things when maybe you haven't seen them. It doesn't help that we were mixing blood in special effects that day. You know, for the battle scenes. Cassius likes them very bloody indeed. Then there was that loud bang the other day when they filmed the handmaiden scene. Just before Patty was arrested. Something's been bugging me about it all.'

'So you're thinking it was fake blood on Patty Carter's dress, which somehow got transferred there?'

'No, because the police would have known it was fake blood, wouldn't they? We're lucky it is fake blood we're using, because Cassius used to like using animal blood until health and safety stopped him. Can you imagine that lot congealing in this heat? Ugh.'

'So what's bothering you?'

'The thing is, I don't know if I'm imagining it all, and with Patty already off at the police station I don't want to get anyone else into trouble.'

'Archer!' They were interrupted by George Cassius. 'Archer, get down to the police station. It seems they're letting Patty go. So she'll need a friend.'

'That's great,' said Matt. 'Yes, I'll go and see if she's okay.'

Olivia doubted that Cassius really cared about whether Patty was alright or not. He only wanted publicity for his film. There would be plenty of that when Matt turned up at the police station. She pulled away from him, becoming sullen in the process.

'We'll talk later,' Matt said to her. 'You can tell me what you're worrying about.'

'Don't bother,' said Olivia, tight-lipped. 'I'm sure Patty needs you much more than I do.'

'I'm just being a friend, Liv.'

'Yeah, whatever.'

Olivia flounced off to the make-up department, and made a great play of moving stuff around whilst not really doing anything other than seething about Matt's apparent need to play the hero for Patty Carter. She liked Patty, because unlike many actresses, she was nice and easy-going. But that did not stop her feeling jealous about the lovely actress's apparent hold on Matt. She pottered around for about ten minutes, trying to stem the tears that threatened to fall.

To take her mind off him, she thought about the problem she had wanted to discuss with him. She had become more and more convinced that there was blood where there should not have been blood. It would be better if she could just ask, 'Why were you covered in blood?'

Despite his despotism, Cassius would also pitch in where needed. He did not make deliberate Hitchcockian appearances in his films, but he had played bit parts when needed, and also prepared and carried props, even though it went against all the union rules. That was the thing about working with George Cassius. Everyone did everything, so Olivia could not say for certain that someone was where they should not have been. It was not a good idea to go around flinging accusations at people when emotions on the set were so high anyway.

After a while she felt thirsty, so she hunted around for her can of pop, and then remembered she had left it on the table next to the vending machine. Hopefully it would have cooled down a bit. It would be a waste of time getting a fresh one if the machine was broken.

She found the can at the far end of the table, which was not where she had left it. She supposed someone had come along and moved it.

She swallowed the drink down in several thirsty gulps — it still tasted vile but at least quenched her thirst momentarily — and then went back to her work.

★   ★   ★

A crowd of reporters waited outside the station, chattering amongst themselves. The chatter became a roar when the doors opened and Patty Carter stepped out on the arm of her solicitor. She had put on a pair of huge sunglasses, and watching from the sidelines, it seemed to Tony that she had suddenly become Jackie Onassis. He wondered who Patty Carter was in the dark, when she thought no one was looking.

He thought during the interview he had glimpsed her, but that woman was gone, and had become someone regal and unapproachable.

The waiting press burst into a cacophony of questions.

'Patty! Patty! Can you tell us why the police have brought you here today?'

'Patty, over here. Did you kill your ex-husband?'

'Patty, is that a Donna Karan sweater that you're wearing?'

Tony stepped forward and put his hand on Patty's shoulder. 'No comment,' she said automatically, before seeming to realise she knew him from somewhere. 'Oh, sorry.'

He pulled her back away from the crowd and spoke in a low voice.

'I understand, Ms Carter. I'm Tony Marcus, and I've been sent here by the insurance agency dealing with the claim for your ex-husband's death. I would like, if possible, to speak to you at some point.'

'I've already told Detective Brady that I don't need the money.'

Tony asked nonchalantly, 'Did you?

There are still some things I would like to know. Could I come and see you in a day or two? At your private residence in Surrey?'

She looked shocked. 'How did you know about that?'

Tony wanted to kick himself. If he let on he had listened in on her interview, it could destroy any case that Sam had against her. And yet, he had to concede, that would make him happy. 'We have it for insurance purposes, of course,' he said quickly.

'Yes, of course, sorry. I suppose you can. Get my number off my solicitor and we'll fix a meeting.'

'Thank you, Ms Carter.'

She turned away.

'You know,' he found himself saying, 'If you need a friend, then I'd be happy to listen.'

She turned back, looking shocked and a little distrustful. 'Why?'

'I don't know. I just thought . . . ' What the hell was he thinking? That he would be Patty Carter's new best friend.

'I'm sure you've got lots of friends.'

She gave him a look he could not fathom. 'Yes, I have friends,' she said, but she did not sound convinced.

At that moment a big black limousine pulled up at the kerb and Matt Archer got out. His appearance caused a flurry of activity amongst the press.

'Patty,' he said, climbing the steps to the police station. 'Come with me, and I'll get you away from all this.'

'Yes, Matt, please do,' she said.

Archer put his arm around her shoulders and led her to the car. The media were so fascinated by this that no one stood in their way or tried to stop them as they got into the car and drove away together.

'Yeah,' said Tony quietly, fighting off intense disappointment. 'You have lots of friends.'

He seethed inwardly. What a fool he was! Thinking he could be her protector. She had obviously cast that role already.

6

'Thanks for the lift, Matt.' The limousine pulled up at the gates of a sprawling villa in Surrey. The centre building was of Georgian design, and it had red brick extensions to either side. White Corinthian columns adorned the façade. The house was reflected in a miniature lake in the front garden, around which the driveway curved, leading to a matching set of gates leading back to the road.

'No problem, Patty. Do you want me to come in with you?'

'No, it's fine.' She changed her mind. 'Actually, yes. Do you mind? Jude will be at school and Mum and Dad are away. I could do with the company.'

'Not at all. I'm here for you if you need me.'

It was a very tempting offer, she thought to herself. Matt was gorgeous. Yet her mind was on the man who had spoken to her at the police station. Tony Marcus, with his jet black hair and startling green eyes. Something had passed between them at the studio, but she also sensed his distrust when he spoke to her. It made her wonder where the offer of being her friend had come from.

'This is a great place,' said Matt, as the gates opened and the limo passed through.

'Yes,' said Patty wistfully. 'It's been a bolthole for me until now. I'm afraid that if the press find out I'm here, I'll get no peace.'

'They won't find out from me.' He took her hand in his. He had nice strong hands. She looked into his blue eyes. It would be nice to keep him around, but she remembered that he was having some sort of fling with Olivia Cooper. Patty had been on the receiving end of unscrupulous females who stole other women's husbands, and she had no intention of doing that to another one of the sisterhood. Besides, she liked Olivia.

'Come on in,' she said, getting out of the car. 'I'll put the kettle on.'

She led him through the house and into an enormous kitchen with units and appliances at one end. This was separated from a cosy living space by a large central island. The kitchen area was white, whilst the living area was different shades of yellow, giving the room a bright, sunshiny feel. 'Tea, coffee or something stronger?' she asked.

'Coffee is fine. Don't you have servants in a big place like this?'

Patty laughed. 'No, I do not. I admit someone comes in to clean every morning. I'm no domestic goddess. I couldn't bear having others living in my house apart from my son and my mum and dad. I have a nanny for Jude, but she has her own flat above the garage and she only comes in here when I'm working.'

'I always said I'd have a place like this,' said Matt, sitting on one of the bar stools that surrounded the island. 'When I made it big.'

'Well now you can.'

'You're kidding,' he laughed. 'One television series and one film, even one directed by George Cassius, does not help a guy to buy a property like this. I've only just about paid off my debts.'

'Ah, yes, sorry, I should have remembered what it was like to be a struggling actor. I've been lucky.'

'So this wasn't Jason's house then?'

'No,' Patty said, pursing her lips. 'I bought it all by myself.'

'Hey, sorry, I didn't mean to be rude.' Matt put up his hands in supplication. 'I just wondered if you'd lived here together.'

'No, we didn't. We lived in Jason's place in L.A. for a while, then we had a house in London; but when we split up, I bought this place. And not with my alimony.'

Matt smiled and nodded courteously. 'Point taken.'

Patty poured the coffee and handed him a cup. 'Do you want to come and sit down?'

'Yeah, sure.'

They went to sit on an overstuffed yellow polka-dot sofa.

'Do you miss Jason?' Matt asked.

Patty sucked in a deep breath. 'It's a strange thing,' she said. 'I think I miss him more because of the way he died than because he's not here. We were good friends. We had to be for our son. But I got used to him not being here. It's the fact that someone did something so awful to him that makes me wish he were still here. I want to ask him why.'

'Who would want to kill him, do you think?'

'I've racked my brains, and I really don't have a clue, Matt.'

'He had lots of ex-wives.'

'Yes, but he stayed friends with all of them. He was that type of man. Even when he was misbehaving you couldn't help but like him. I can't see any of them wanting to kill him to get revenge on his cheating. And it's not as if any of his exes would benefit from him dying.'

'But you do?'

Patty glanced at him sharply. 'Jude does.'

'Jude?'

'Our son.'

'Oh yeah. Do you know, I didn't know his name till you just said? You don't talk about him much. How come he never comes to the studio?'

'Where his father died?' Patty raised an eyebrow.

'I mean before that.'

'Jason and I agreed to keep him away from that world as much as we could. You know yourself that show business is completely fake. It's almost like a parallel world where things happen a bit differently to how they do in the real world. Huge stars can get away with murder — literally — or other crimes and still be lauded. We wanted our son to have a chance to grow up with a good moral outlook. If he decides he wants to act sometime in the future, that's fine. As long as he understands by then that Hollywood life and real life are two different things.'

The slamming of the front door, the thunder of feet and the chatter of voices interrupted them. Jude came bounding into the kitchen, followed by a homely-looking middle-aged woman. Jude was like a male version of his mother, with dark hair and violet eyes.

On seeing Patty was there with a visitor, the woman smiled and made a discreet exit. 'Thanks, Hannah,' Patty called.

'Hello, mum. I thought you were filming.' Jude was about to run to his mother, then noticed Matt. He stopped suddenly. Patty guessed that he would not want to appear soppy and kiss his mother in front of a man.

'This is Matt Archer, Jude.'

'Hello,' said Jude, his eyes narrowing suspiciously.

'Matt Archer from *The Last Gladiator*?' said Patty, grinning.

'Oh wow,' said Jude. 'Mum won't let me watch it, though I've seen some at my friend's house. It's brill.' That was news to Patty and she made a note to have a chat with the mother of Jude's friend. *The Last Gladiator* was not suitable for children.

Jude held out his hand politely.

'Hey, Jude,' said Matt, shaking his hand.

Jude rolled his eyes. 'I've heard that three million times already. The Beatles, 'Hey Jude' and all that . . . '

'Sorry, cobber. Nice to meet you.'

'You're Australian.' Jude's eyes widened.

'That's right.'

'Wow, but you talk with such a good British accent in *The Last Gladiator*.'

'I don't think they had many Australian gladiators,' Patty quipped.

'That's so the Yanks can understand me,' said Matt.

'Yeah,' said Jude. 'Their English is really strange, isn't it?'

'Oh yeah.'

'Are you staying for tea, Matt? If you are, I can show you my *Star Wars* figures.'

'Oh, I'm sure Matt has other things to do,' said Patty.

69

'Some other time, cobber,' said Matt. He put his cup down on the coffee table, a little bit too quickly. Patty noticed that he was not unkind to Jude. Just a little disinterested and perhaps alarmed at being pounced upon as Jude's new best friend so quickly. Matt must think she was trying to ensnare a father for her son. 'I should be getting back to the studio.'

Jude's face dropped. 'Okay,' he said.

Matt stood up. 'Thanks for the coffee, Patty.'

She got up and led him out to the front door, leaving Jude rummaging in the fridge for a snack. 'He's a great kid,' Matt said.

'Yes he is. He does want to be everyone's best friend though, so I hope he didn't make you feel too awkward in there.'

'No, not at all. I just thought you might want to be alone with him.' Good recovery, thought Patty.

'Yes, thanks. I need to explain a few things to him.'

Patty had just opened the front door when Matt's mobile phone rang. He listened avidly, his normally cheerful face falling. 'Jesus . . . ' he whispered. Patty thought he was going to keel over, so she caught him by the arm and led him to a chair in the hallway.

'What is it?' she asked when he had put the phone down.

'It's Olivia,' he said, his voice barely above a whisper. 'She's dead.'

7

Jude sat up in bed, reading a book. 'Someone else died today, didn't they, mum?' he asked. 'I saw it on the news.'

Patty finished folding his clothes and then perched on the edge of his bed. 'Yes. Olivia Cooper, the make-up girl. She was really nice and I think Matt liked her a lot.'

'Do you have to go back?' His sweet little face took on a worried air.

'I don't know, darling. I'm under contract and it would cost me a lot of money to break it. I suppose it depends if the producers decide to cancel the whole thing.'

'It's very interesting really, isn't it?' he asked, matter-of-factly.

Patty looked startled. 'What? People dying? Your father dying?'

'I'm really sorry about dad, but I'm also interested about who would want to kill him and the others. Aren't you?'

'I'd like to know so they can be arrested and then we can get on with our lives.'

'Dad left me lots of money, didn't he?'

'Ye-es,' said Patty, frowning. It was not the sort of thing that Jude normally cared about.

'Well, if you didn't go back to the studio and they sued you for it, like they did with Kim Basinger when she didn't want to do that film, I could pay them off for you with dad's money.'

She stroked his dark hair. 'You'd do that for me?'

'Dad would want me to keep you safe. He loved you, you know. He told me.'

'Did he?' Patty swallowed back a lump in her throat.

'He said he was an idiot to let you go. I told him he was too.'

Patty laughed and fought back a stray tear. 'I bet you did.'

'Is Matt Archer going to be your boyfriend?'

'Oh, I don't think so, sweetheart.' She kissed him on the head. 'You're not going to lose me, whatever happens. I promise.'

'Mum?'

'What, sweetie?'

'Why do the police think you killed Dad?'

'I think it's because they have no other suspects at the moment.' Patty looked at her son squarely. 'Aren't you going to ask me if I did?'

'I don't need to. I already know the answer. I'm going to go to sleep now.' Jude put his book down and snuggled under the duvet.

Patty wanted to ask him what he thought the answer was, but she also knew that when her son decided he did not want to talk anymore, it was impossible to draw him out. She kissed him and went to turn out the bedroom light. 'I love you, darling,' she said.

'Okay.' She knew him well enough to know that it was his way of saying he loved her too. He was at the age where to admit loving one's mother was severely frowned upon by his peers.

She went to the kitchen and poured herself a glass of merlot, taking a long sip. She started to clear away the dinner dishes, all the time thinking about Jason and the other deaths at the studio. Surely the police would not suspect her when two other people had died whilst she was elsewhere? Unless they thought the deaths were unconnected.

Matt had been stunned by the news of Olivia's death. As he was leaving he had given Patty a strange, confused look. It made her think of all the questions he had asked her about Jason. Did he think she had killed her ex-husband too? She wondered if he had only pretended to come to her aid, in order to find out the truth.

She had just finished putting the dishes into the dishwasher when a bell rang, telling her someone was at the front gate. She went to the small monitor at the side of the front door and also switched on the floodlight over the gate. It was Tony Marcus, standing outside his car looking up at the CCTV camera.

Patty pressed the intercom button. 'I thought you were going to make an appointment, Mr Marcus,' she said sternly, resenting his intrusion into her private space. Yet she was also curious about him.

'I'm sorry, Ms Carter, but I really need to speak to you and it can't wait. My bosses need an answer from me.'

'Tell your bosses that I don't answer to them.'

'Surely you want this sorted out to your son's advantage, Ms Carter?'

Patty bristled. 'Actually . . . ' She bit her lip. Maybe it was best to get it over with. She pressed another button and the electronic gates started to open. She watched as Tony Marcus got into his sleek sports car and drove up to the house. She pressed the button to shut the gates, and waited by the front door.

'Come in,' she said, when he had parked the car and walked up to the porch. There was something about his presence that unnerved her. With Matt she had felt relaxed, at least until the news about Olivia came, but with Tony Marcus she felt on edge. 'Come to the kitchen. We can talk there without waking my son.'

'I'm sorry if I've disturbed you, Ms Carter.'

'Somehow I doubt that,' Patty said briskly, as she passed through into the kitchen. 'Otherwise you wouldn't have come. Can I offer you a drink, Mr Marcus?'

'No, thank you. I'm driving.'

'Tea then? Or coffee?'

'Actually I'd like a decent cup of British tea. They just don't know how to do it in the States.'

'Tell me about it,' said Patty, forcing herself to be graceful when all she wanted to do was scream at him to get the hell out of her house. 'Take a seat and I'll bring it to you.' She gestured to the sofa. As the night had drawn cold, she had lit the wood-burning stove. It gave off a cosy glow.

'No servants?'

'You're the second person to ask me that today. Why does everyone assume that an actress is incapable of making her own tea?'

'It's just that this is a big place.'

'We manage.'

'You and your son ... er ... Jude, isn't it?'

'That's right.' She felt no urge to elaborate.

She finished making the tea and brought a tray over to the coffee table. 'Since you've missed British tea, I assumed you might miss chocolate digestives too. Help yourself.'

Tony smiled. He had a stunning smile and it occurred to Patty that he could easily be an actor. He certainly had the looks for it. She sat down on one of the easy chairs and curled her legs under her. 'So tell me, Mr Marcus, did you go to Hollywood in search of stardom and then end up working as a private detective when the roles didn't come?'

'No, I was a policeman before I went to the States.' His green eyes darkened. 'I needed a change of scenery so I gave up my job in the force and went to America. I'd always loved the Philip Marlowe stories so I decided to set up as a private detective.'

'Do you get many red-headed femme fatales through your door?'

'Not nearly enough.' He frowned. 'But I think I'm supposed to be questioning you.'

'Go ahead. I'm not sure how I can help you though. Your friend, Detective Brady, knows how my ex-husband died.'

'Yes, it must have been awful for you to find him like that.'

'You couldn't begin to imagine,' said Patty. She felt tired. She had talked over Jason's death so many times with the police and with Hannah, the nanny who had taken care of her when she returned home stricken to tell her son what had happened to his father. Her parents had phoned, but had been unable to return home. They had a play to do and the show must go on, as they said in showbiz circles.

'Actually, I could. I lost someone close to me before I went to America. Not in the same circumstances, but it was still tragic.'

'I'm sorry to hear that. Is that the real reason you went?'

'Yes, I suppose it was.'

'You must have loved her very much.'

'Actually it was a he.'

'Oh.' Patty wondered how to proceed, especially as she had an unaccountable feeling of disappointment. 'Then you must have loved him very much.'

'I did.' He smiled sadly. 'You can stop panicking about how you're going to deal with a delicate situation, Ms Carter. It was my elder brother.'

'Oh. I am sorry.' Was it relief she felt? 'How did he die?'

'My brother was into extreme sports, much to the chagrin of my mother and father. He was abseiling off a cliff when his rope broke. He was only twenty-eight.'

'That's awful.'

'Yes, it hit Mum and Dad pretty hard too.'

'They must have felt as though they'd lost both of you when you went to America.'

Tony harrumphed awkwardly. 'I hadn't thought of it like that.'

'Have you seen them since you got back?'

'No, no, I haven't had a chance.'

'Well you should go, you know. Family is important.'

'Yes, you're right, it is.' He started to laugh. 'We seem to have ended up talking more about me than you, Ms Carter.'

'Call me Patty. Ms Carter makes me sound like a headmistress. And you're Tony, right? Unless you'd prefer Mr Marcus.'

'Tony is fine.'

'Anyway, you're not here to talk about me, are you? You're here to talk about Jason. And as I've said, the cause of his death was obvious to anyone. I don't know how the insurance people could be confused.'

'If he was killed for that money . . . '

'Oh, I see. Yes, there is that I suppose. But my son is the only one who benefits and he didn't kill his father. He has an alibi in the shape of a maths test that very morning. He did very well on it too,' she added proudly.

'I'm sure your son is innocent. But there are other confusing elements.'

'What's confusing about a knife sticking out of a man's chest?' Patty asked, bitterness rising in her chest.

'Jason Carter was said to be a hell-raiser, yet there was no trace of alcohol or drugs in his blood. Nothing at all. And his liver was as clean as a whistle. If he had been a heavy drinker, there would have been scarring.'

'And this is a bad thing, why?'

'He was known to have, shall we say, episodes, where he shook uncontrollably. People generally thought it was the effects of his drinking. Now it's clear it can't have been that. So my employers want to know if he had been completely honest when filling in his medical history.'

'As I was not there when he filled in the forms, I couldn't possibly tell you,' said Patty in a prim voice. 'Jason was my ex-husband. We got on well, for the sake of our son, but we did not live together and I have no personal knowledge of his dealings with the insurers.'

'But as his ex-wife, you would know if he suffered from any illnesses.'

'Why? We separated over ten years ago and divorced very soon after that. He had four wives after me. Or was it five? I lose track to be honest, especially as he was married to one of them for three whole hours after a mad dash to Las Vegas. Why don't you ask one of them? They're all in America. It would have saved you the trip.'

'We have, and they're all doing what you're doing. They're clamming up. So you can imagine why we feel suspicious. He must have been quite a man to engender so much loyalty.'

'My ex-husband was a flawed man, but it did not make him a bad man. He was capable of great kindness and generosity. In fact, it was his generosity that got him into so much trouble.' Patty grinned wryly but there was no humour in her tone. 'He couldn't say no to anyone.'

'That must have hurt you a lot.'

'It did ten years ago. I know everyone has theories about a woman scorned and all that, Mr Marcus.'

'Tony.'

'But we don't all become murderous when wronged by our men . . . Tony. Perhaps you need to make up your mind. Either I murdered my ex-husband, or I'm hiding something about him.'

'Maybe it's both.'

Patty put her glass of wine down on the table with a thump. 'I've said all I can say. If you don't mind, I'd like to get some rest.'

'Patty, I'm sorry. There is a huge question now over whether you murdered your ex-husband, unless there are two murderers at the studio, and that seems very unlikely. The girl, Olivia, was poisoned by a drink that she bought from a vending machine in full sight of everyone whilst you were at the police station. You have the best alibi there is.'

'You seem to know a lot about this.'

'Sam Brady is an old friend. He let me know as soon as they received news of Olivia's death.'

'It's all completely mad,' said Patty, picking up her drink again. She felt close to tears, yet she had not been able to cry at all since Jason's death. 'All this murder at the studio. My son doesn't want me to go back there. He's even said he'll use his father's inheritance to pay them off if they sue me. He's ten years old and he shouldn't even be worrying about these things. Why aren't the producers pulling the plug?' The question was rhetorical. She doubted that Tony Marcus would know.

'They probably will now. Cassius is bound to halt production.'

'You don't know George Cassius.

The man is mad. They say he's a genius, which is why we all want to work with him, but he's absolutely crazy. I'm telling you, that man could turn straw into gold. Like he did when the actor died in his remake of *Ben Hur*. The film was dreadful, yet millions went to see it in the hopes of seeing the point at which that poor actor's head was knocked from his body. And Cassius played on that, by hinting that he may have left the scene in.'

'I hear this film is his last chance to make good with Hollywood.'

'So I've heard. I wouldn't put it past him to have committed these murders himself. He's mad enough to see it as part of his fictive dream.'

'He'd have a job convincing actors to work with him in the future.'

'I don't think George cares,' said Patty. 'He wants to be a legend, and he doesn't care how he gets there.'

'Mum?' Jude entered the kitchen wearing his *Star Wars* pyjamas.

Patty turned around startled. 'Hello,

darling. I thought you were asleep.'

'I heard you talking. Is this another boyfriend?'

'No,' said Patty, flustered. *Another boyfriend?* What on earth must Tony Marcus think of her? 'This is Mr Marcus. He's a private investigator. Tony, this is my son, Jude.'

'Glad to meet you, Jude,' said Tony, holding out his hand.

Jude smiled and walked to the seating area to accept the handshake. Patty instinctively knew he was pleased that Tony had not said 'Hey Jude' like everyone else did when they met him. 'You're a real private investigator?' asked Jude, wide-eyed. 'Not an actor or anything?'

'Not an actor. I used to be a policeman and now I'm a P.I.'

'Wicked,' said Jude, sitting on the sofa next to Tony. 'Do you carry a gun?'

'Not in Britain. It isn't allowed.'

'But you do in America?'

'If I need to, yes.'

'That is so rad. Have you ever shot anyone?'

'Jude!' Patty exclaimed. 'What a dreadful thing to ask.'

'I wouldn't brag about it if I did,' said Tony in grave tones. Patty could not help noticing that the corners of his mouth twitched in amusement.

'Are you trying to find out who killed my dad?' asked Jude.

'No, that isn't my reason for being here,' said Tony. 'I'm just investigating your father's medical history.'

'Is that all?' Jude flashed Tony a look of intense disappointment. 'I thought you were here to help us.'

'I would like to help if I can,' said Tony.

'No you won't. You don't really care. You're just saying that. The police have got it all wrong anyway. Mum didn't do it.'

'I'm sure she didn't.'

'They're really stupid, especially that detective who questioned mum.'

'Jude,' said Patty, trying to be stern when she really wanted to laugh. 'Detective Brady is Mr Marcus's friend.'

'Well he's still stupid,' said Jude. 'I've already worked out what's going on.'

'Really?' said Tony, his eyes crinkling with amusement. 'Care you share your thoughts, Jude? We need all the help we can get, and if we can get an expert . . . '

'If you're just going to make fun, I shan't bother.' Jude stood up. 'I'm going back to bed, mum.'

'Come here,' said Patty. She stood up and gave her son a hug, kissing the top of his head. 'We'll talk about it tomorrow and you can share your thoughts with me then, when we're alone. I won't make fun, I promise.'

'Jude, I'm sorry, mate,' said Tony. 'I didn't mean to make fun. I would be interested in hearing what you have to say. It really might help.'

Patty cast him a suspicious glance. Did he think that Jude might have something against her?

'Well . . . ' said Jude, hesitantly. 'Have you noticed how everyone who's been murdered has died in the same way as their characters in the film?' Jude's words hung in the air momentarily as Patty and Tony grasped the significance.

'How do you mean?' Tony finally asked.

'Dad was playing Julius Caesar, right?'

'Yes, darling,' said Patty. She sat down and pulled Jude onto her knee. His little body trembled, which worried her greatly. She prayed it was just nerves, especially whilst Tony Marcus was in the house.

'Well, Julius Caesar was stabbed to death. By Brutus and all them, wasn't he?' Jude warmed to his theme. 'Then that other man, Andy Paxton, who played Cleopatra's manservant, he died of poison. And that's how the manservant died. Then Olivia, who was sort of a hand-maiden to mum, because she did all her make-up and everything, was poisoned. And they've got the same initials as characters from the films. Dad is . . . was . . . J.C. like Julius Caesar. Andy Paxton is A like Appolodorus, and Olivia is O like Octavia, even though she didn't die in the film.'

'Yes, that's exactly right,' said Tony. 'I can see I underestimated you, Jude. I'm sorry about that.'

'But that's why you have to help us, Mr Marcus,' said Jude, his dark eyes wider than ever. 'And why I hoped you've got a gun and you're not afraid to use it. Because if I am right, then it means that someone will try to kill mummy, maybe even with a snake in a basket or something like Cleopatra died in the first film.'

8

'Jude,' said Patty quietly, 'I think you should calm down now, darling.' She hugged him to her whilst Tony watched, perplexed. The child's whole body was shaking. 'Please,' she whispered. 'Please try not to get too upset.'

'But mum . . .'

'I know, I know,' she whispered, pulling him to her and holding him tightly. Her eyes, which were so much like her son's, filled with tears. 'I know, baby.'

'What's wrong?' said Tony. Something was going on, and he suspected it had little to do with Jude's revelation. Or maybe it was a part of it, but there was something else.

'Could you leave now, please?' asked Patty. 'Jude and I need to be alone.'

'He's ill.'

'No!' The word shot out like a bullet

from a gun. 'He is not ill! He is fine. Or he will be if you just go away. He's had too much stress lately, that's all.' She turned to look at her son. 'Jude?'

Suddenly Jude's body went rigid and his eyes rolled into the back of his head. Patty almost dropped him, and Tony jumped up to help her catch him as he crumbled to the floor.

'What can I do?' he asked.

'Go away and leave us be!'

'Patty, I want to help. Does he need anything? Any medication? A doctor? An ambulance?'

'No, it will pass soon. He just needs peace and quiet and God knows he's had little of that lately.' She hugged Jude to her, stroking his hair. 'It's alright, my darling, let it go. Let it go now . . . shh . . . '

Gradually, after what seemed like a lifetime to Tony, Jude's body relaxed and his eyes fluttered. 'Oh mummy, I'm sorry,' he sobbed, tears filling his eyes.

'Oh no, no, my darling,' she said, kissing his face. In that moment, Tony thought he saw the real Patty Carter. Not the actress, not the queen of Egypt or Helen of Troy or Joan of Arc, but a devoted mother who would do anything for her child. He wished he could find comfort in that, but he was not so sure. Just how far would she go to ensure her son had a good life? 'You never have to be sorry. Never,' she told Jude. She glanced up at Tony. 'If you'd really like to help, could you fetch some water please? There are bottles in the fridge.'

Tony went to the massive American-style fridge-freezer and found the mineral water, bringing it back to Patty. He twisted the lid off and gave it to her and she helped Jude to drink some.

'Epilepsy?' he said.

'Yes,' she replied. 'But he was getting better, weren't you, baby?' she said, smiling. 'Nearly two years without an attack and then all this. I knew it was only a matter of time.'

'I should think losing his dad would do that.'

'He's been fighting it though, haven't

you, darling? Or hiding it.'

'I had an attack the other day,' said Jude. 'But I told Hannah not to tell you.'

'I know.'

'She wasn't supposed to say.' He sounded indignant.

'She has to tell me, sweetheart. I'm your mother.'

'But it was our secret.'

'Don't be mad at her. She loves you nearly as much as I do.'

Jude looked up at Tony, who was crouched on the floor near to them. 'Will you make sure no one hurts my mum, Mr Marcus? I'll pay you. I've got some savings and my dad left me some money. He'd want us to take care of her.'

'Mr Marcus is a busy man, darling, and it would be a conflict of interest for him to help us.'

'What does that mean?' asked Jude.

'It means he can't work for us and for the people who are paying him at the moment.'

'That doesn't mean I can't look into what Jude has said,' said Tony. 'Jason won't be the only one claiming from the insurance company. They will want to know what happened.'

'What? So they can find other reasons not to pay out?' Patty raised an eyebrow. For the first time ever, he felt ashamed of what he did.

'I thought the money didn't matter,' he said.

Her eyes narrowed and he remembered that he was not supposed to know that about her. 'It doesn't for me,' she said. 'But I imagine it will for Andy Paxton and Olivia's family. They aren't as well off as we are.'

'I'm sure that the insurance company won't use what's happened as an excuse not to pay them out.' He emphasised the 'them', because he was beginning to get an inkling why Patty Carter was being defensive about Jason Carter. He would need to investigate more to be certain, but it was all falling into place. The main question was, why would she hide the truth? Was it for the money or for some other reason?

'I see,' she said, and he guessed that she did see. 'Would you mind seeing yourself out, Mr Marcus? I'm going to put my son to bed.'

He was no longer Tony to her. She had become distant again.

'Do you need any help?'

'No, we're fine, aren't we darling?' she said, smiling a bit too brightly at her son.

'Yes, mum. We don't need anyone else, do we?' said Jude.

Tony felt a pang of sadness. For a few minutes Jude had looked at him as if he were a hero. He wondered why he missed it now it was gone. He owed nothing to Jude or to his mother and yet he felt guilty for letting them both down.

'Hey, Jude,' he said, and was answered with a withering look. It took him a second or two to realise why. 'Sorry. I didn't mean to say it like the song. I just want to promise you that I won't let anything happen to your mum. Okay?'

'You can't work for us.'

'No, I can't work for you. But I can take care of my friends, can't I?'

'Yes, I suppose so.'

'Great, so I'll ask around and find out what's going on.'

'Will you share your findings with me?' asked Jude, managing to sound mature and childlike at the same time. Tony recognised that he was being given a sacred trust.

Tony nodded. 'I will certainly do that, pal. Then you can help me work things out. But you have to share your findings with me, too.'

'What can I do to help?' asked Jude, looking proud.

'You could look on the internet and see what you can find out about the people who died. Not your dad, of course, because you already know about him.'

'That's good,' said Jude. 'Because you should always look at the victim to help find out who killed them. Poirot says that.'

'Yep, that's how it's done,' said Tony.

'I can see we're going to work great together.'

Patty stood up and helped Jude to his feet. 'Come on, Watson,' she said, her lips twitching at the corners. Despite her amusement, her eyes were dark and troubled. 'Let Sherlock get off home. He doesn't have school in the morning, but you do.' She turned to Tony. 'You know where the front door is? The control for the gate is there. It should close automatically after you've gone through.'

'Okay, thanks.'

She took Jude out into the hallway, and Tony followed. Jude had quickly got over his seizure and was talking excitedly.

'I like him,' he said to his mother. 'Now he's going to help us, I mean. He's a real person, isn't he, mum?'

'Of course he's a real person.'

'No, I mean, Matt Archer is cool and all that, but he's not a real gladiator. He only pretends to be one on the telly. Mr Marcus is a real private eye, and he has a gun in America. He's our friend now, so I know everything will be okay.'

'Jude ... ' Patty's voice fell to a murmur, but Tony heard the initial warning note. Unfortunately, whatever else she said to her son was too low for him to hear, but he guessed she was cautioning the child not to rely too heavily on him. Nevertheless, he was glad that he scored higher on Jude's likeability chart than Matt Archer.

He watched them walk up the stairs and disappear around a corner, and then he took his phone out of his pocket. As he dialled, he went to the front door and found the controls to the gate that Patty had mentioned.

'Yeah, it's Tony Marcus,' he said when the person at the other end answered. 'I want you to look something up for me. It's about Jason Carter. I want his entire medical history. Find out which doctors he saw and when . . . in Britain and the States if you can. Let me know when you have it all.'

Tony opened the front door and

stepped out. At first he thought the sudden rush of light was from the security system. Then he saw the reporters starting to surge towards the gates and realised that the light was the flash of a dozen or more cameras.

Tony dashed back into the house and hit the button for the gates, and then he ran back outside to make sure it was closing. As if realising they could get trapped and might be in a lot of trouble for trespassing, the reporters moved back onto the public footpath, behind the security gates.

He went back into the house just as Patty was coming down the stairs.

'You've got a problem,' he said.

'What is it?'

'There are a dozen or more reporters outside, along with several television crews.'

Her hands flew to her mouth. 'How did they get here? I don't give this address out to anyone and I'm always careful I'm not followed.' She looked at him accusingly.

'I promise it wasn't me, Patty. I guess they can look up the property records.'

She sat down on the stairs, as if defeated by the problem. 'No, I own the house through a holding company, which is listed to a post office box in London. Someone must have told them.' She ran her hands through her hair. 'I have to get Jude out of here. But how?'

It was not Tony's problem. That was what he told himself. Yet something about her made him long to take her up in his arms and protect her. She looked so vulnerable sitting on the stairs. Completely different to the cool, calm and collected woman who had deflected all his questions in the kitchen. 'I can take you away in my car.'

'No, thank you. I could drive out if I wanted to, but I can't take Jude through all those flashing cameras.'

'Of course, I see.' He vaguely remembered warnings about flashing images on television. 'Is there any other way out?'

'We could try to go through the

neighbour's garden. The one that backs onto mine. They're away, but that doesn't solve the problem of what we do when we reach the road.'

'I'll leave by the front gate and come around and collect you.'

'What if they follow you? They're bound to want to know who you are.'

'Yes, that is a problem.' Tony rubbed his chin thoughtfully. 'How big is your back garden?'

'What?' Patty frowned, looking confused. 'What has that got to do with anything?'

'How big is it? I mean, could a helicopter land safely in it?'

'Yes, I suppose so. In fact there's a double-width tennis court. One could probably land there quite easily. But I don't know anyone with a helicopter.'

'I do,' said Tony. 'You just get Jude ready and pack some clothes.'

Patty stood up again, but hesitantly. 'But I don't know where to go.'

'What about your folks' house? Or some friends?'

'My parents normally live here with us when they're not travelling in repertory theatre. At this moment they're staying in a guest house in North Wales while they're starring in an Agatha Christie play. As for friends . . . I don't really have many proper friends. Only those in the business, and I don't entirely trust them all.'

'Sounds lonely,' said Tony.

'I didn't mean to sound like a poor little rich girl.' Her small chin jutted upwards again. 'I'm quite capable of surviving.'

'Yeah, you're doing really well at the moment,' he said, wryly, jerking his head in the direction of the reporters at the gate. It earned him a sharp look.

'Thank you for your offer of help, Mr Marcus, but Jude and I will be fine here for tonight. I'll contact the police and let them know there could be trouble. Then tomorrow, when my son is rested, I'll book us into a hotel.'

'No, look, I want to help. It is possible, I suppose, that the reporters heard us talking today and then followed me, so I may be partly responsible for them being here.' He did not think that was the case, but he was determined she would let him help her. 'You get ready and I'll arrange the chopper. Will it be alright if I leave my car here for a day or two?'

'Erm, yes. I don't suppose I have much choice, do I? I don't want Jude bothered by those people. But where will we go?'

'I'll sort something out.'

*   *   *

It was nearly midnight when the helicopter landed on a large patch of land in the Peak District. Jude had loved every moment of the ride, looking out excitedly at the lights of Britain below them. He had travelled in a plane, but never in a helicopter. Patty noted, with some concern, that it only increased his sudden hero-worship of Tony.

'Leave the bags. I'll get someone to fetch them up,' Tony told them as they were landing.

'Where are we?' Jude called to Tony when they had disembarked and were out of the way of the rotor blades.

'This is my home,' Tony called back. 'But I haven't been here for ages. So be prepared for the fatted calf and all that.'

'Will they mind us turning up?' asked Patty. As she spoke, the chopper engine died, leaving her shouting out in the quiet night. 'Sorry,' she murmured, afraid she had disturbed the residents of the big imposing house to which they were headed.

Tony smiled. 'Don't worry. They'll be awake anyway.'

'Wow,' said Jude, 'is this a hotel?'

It was difficult to make the house out in the dark. It loomed over them. Patty wondered what it would look like in daylight.

'Nope,' said Tony. 'It's a house. Well, more of a palace really.'

As they climbed one side of a set of

curved steps that traversed the front of the house, the front door opened and a man who looked to be in his late fifties or early sixties stepped out, illuminated by the light from the inside hallway. Jude took Patty's hand, and she sensed he was a little bit afraid. But the man just smiled benignly at them, and then at Tony Marcus.

'Welcome home, Lord Anthony.'

9

Patty was still digesting the information about Tony's noble status as they entered the house. Patty's home in Surrey was large enough, but she still guessed that at least half of it would fit into the grand hallway of Tony's home. They stood on a *piano nobile*, just inside the front door, looking down at it.

'Welcome to Fazeby Hall,' he said to her, as she stood transfixed by the history that appeared before her. She guessed that the house was probably Tudor in origin. A massive central staircase led to a minstrels' gallery that surrounded the whole upper floor and joined to staircases at either side of the *piano nobile*. They took a few steps down into the hallway.

'Wow,' said Jude. 'This is brilliant.'

'I'm glad you like it,' said Tony, smiling. There was some sadness in his eyes, and Patty wondered why.

'The Duke and Duchess are waiting in the drawing room,' said the butler. *Duke and Duchess?* Patty looked at Tony, disbelievingly.

'Thank you, Stephens.' As Tony spoke, double doors to the side of the hall opened and a man and woman came out. The man was an older version of Tony, with hair greying at the temples. He looked to be about seventy. The woman was younger, perhaps in her late fifties or early sixties, but she was still very beautiful. She ran forward and embraced him. 'Anthony, my darling,' she said, with tears filling her pretty blue eyes. 'I'm so glad you've come home.'

'Even if it is rather late,' said the Duke, with a smile. Patty sensed that he too wanted to hug his son, but some constraint — perhaps male pride — stopped him.

'It's good to see you, sir,' said Tony, holding out his hand, when his mother had finally let him go. The Duke shook his hand and it seemed as if they were strangers just meeting.

'Aren't you going to introduce us to our guests?' said the Duchess.

'Yes, of course,' said Tony. 'Forgive my bad manners.'

Patty frowned. It was as if he had become a different person. The easy-going air he had as a private investigator had disappeared and was replaced by someone much more formal. She suspected he was not entirely comfortable in their surroundings.

'Mum, Dad, this is Patty Carter and her son, Jude. As I explained on the phone, they need a place to hide out for a day or two. Patty, Jude, this is my father, Harry, Duke of Fazeby and my mother, Diana, Duchess of Fazeby.'

'We're very glad to meet you both,' said Diana, smiling warmly at Patty. 'I am sorry for your recent loss.'

'Thank you,' said Patty, feeling some of the constraint that Tony felt. How did one behave in front of a duke and duchess? She had only ever met the nobility in formal situations, at gala performances. 'Your Grace,' she added, as an afterthought.

'Oh, we don't stand on ceremony here,' said Diana, giving another flash of her warm smile. 'Not with guests. I'm Diana, and this is Harry. And I hope that we may call you Patty and Jude.'

'Yes, of course,' said Patty, impressed by the way Diana instantly knew how to put people at their ease. It was something she had never learned as an actress, and at times it made appearing in public an ordeal. She was much more comfortable hiding behind a role.

'Now, you must have tea and toast, and then we'll get Stephens to show you to your rooms. We've put you and Jude in adjoining rooms, as I'm sure you'll want to keep him near to you.'

'Thank you, you're very kind,' said Patty. Jude had not spoken a word. He was even more overwhelmed by their surroundings than Patty.

They followed Diana and Harry into

the drawing room, where within minutes Stephens arrived with a tray of tea things. With him came a homely-looking woman carrying a plate full of toast and fresh scones. They set the food and drink down on the coffee table and made a discreet exit.

It was all very civilised and for a while, as everyone sized each other up, all that could be heard was the gentle clink of crockery.

'This is the best toast ever,' said Jude, finding his voice at last. 'And the butter is the tastiest ever.'

'We make it here on the estate, Jude,' said Diana. 'Mrs Stephens is a treasure. I don't know what we'd do without either of them actually. Mr Stephens has worked for the Fazeby family for years, and he took over from his father before him and so on. In fact, they've probably got more claim to Fazeby Hall than the Fazeby family.'

'The way things are going, they'll have it,' said Harry, darkly.

'Don't start,' said Tony. A nerve

twitched in his jaw.

'No, don't start,' said Diana, mildly. 'Not when we have guests.'

Patty put her cup down, still feeling awkward. There was so much hanging in the air, unsaid, between Tony and his father. She began to worry that Fazeby Hall might not have been the best place to bring Jude, with so much underlying tension between father and son. 'Thank you so much for welcoming us into your home,' she said. 'I really ought to put Jude to bed.'

'Of course,' said Diana. 'The poor child must be exhausted. I'll get Stephens to show you the way. If you need any-thing, just ring down to the kitchen and they'll provide it.'

'I don't think I'll sleep, mum,' said Jude. 'I'm too excited. How old is the house, sir?' he asked Harry. The duke looked delighted to be asked.

'It's about six hundred years old in all. It used to be a Norman manor house, and then it was rebuilt in Tudor times. It's been in the Fazeby family all that time.' He was looking at Tony as he spoke. 'But sadly it looks as though when I'm gone it will just be sold off for scrap.'

'No!' said Jude. 'That can't happen. Tony won't let it. Will you, Tony?'

Tony looked down studiously at his cup of tea. The air bristled with unspoken rancour, and Patty's heart went out to Diana, who was clearly trying to keep things cheerful.

'I think,' said Patty, suspecting that Jude was treading on dangerous ground, 'we should get you to bed, Jude. I'm sure Tony has a lot to catch up on with his parents.'

'Can I see the rest of the house tomorrow?' Jude asked. He looked from Tony to Harry, and then to Diana, as if unsure whom he should be asking. 'Because normally when we go to stately homes we're only allowed to see bits and there's red rope everywhere. I'd like a real look around, if I can, please. I promise not to break anything.'

'Of course you can look around,

Jude,' said Diana, laughing. 'I'll tell you all about Fazeby Hall during the Civil War, shall I?'

'Oh yes, please,' said Jude. 'We're doing about Cromwell at school. Oh . . . ' he turned to Patty. 'What about school, Mummy?'

'I'll telephone them in the morning and explain your absence,' said Patty. 'Come on, sweetheart.' She stood up and smiled at Diana.

'We'd best phone Sam Brady too,' said Tony.

'Yes, of course. I can't have him thinking I'm running off.'

'Tony's friend thinks that mummy murdered my dad,' Jude explained to Diana, with all the innocence of youth. Because he did not believe it, it did not occur to him that anyone else would. 'But we know that's not true because other people are dying. So Tony is going to look after us, and keep us safe. I suppose that's why we're here, so we're awfully grateful to you for letting us stay, Duke and Duchess.'

The Duke smiled for the first time that evening. Jude's enthusiasm for everything always was infectious. 'Then we'll help him to make sure no harm comes to either of you,' he said.

'I hope you and Tony make up your argument too,' said Jude, ignoring Patty's gasp of horror. 'Because I know what it's like to lose a dad and it's not nice. You should really stick together.'

'Come on,' Patty whispered. 'This is really none of our business.' She mouthed sorry to the Duke and Duchess and took Jude out into the hallway. Stephens, who was obviously well trained, was already waiting to show them upstairs.

As they followed Stephens up the stairs, Patty heard Tony say in a low, bitter voice, 'Aren't you going to say something about me bringing a possible murderer into your house?' Her cheeks flamed scarlet. She did not hear Harry and Diana's response, but she did not need to. Tony's feelings about her were bad enough. She fought a compulsion to grab Jude and just run out of the

116

door. She did not know how she was going to be able to face the duke and duchess in the morning.

She followed Stephens to a bedroom in the west wing of the house. He opened the door and let her in, switching on the light as he did so. Then he went to another door inside the bedroom and opened that.

'The young master can sleep in there,' he said. 'Is there anything else you need, Ms Carter?'

'Oh, our clothes . . . '

'Have all been unpacked for you. That door,' he pointed to the corner of the room, 'leads to the bathroom. You should find all the toiletries you need in there, but if you require anything else, just ask.'

'I'm sure we'll be fine. Thank you, Mr Stephens.'

'It's just Stephens, ma'am. I'll wish you goodnight.'

When he had gone, Patty took a better look at the room. It was dominated by a massive four-poster bed. Jude ran across the room and dived onto it. 'Mum, this is brilliant, isn't it?'

'Yes, it is rather wonderful,' she said.

'And toast and scones with tea for supper. It's like being in *Downton Abbey*. Why don't we ever have toast and cake for supper?'

'Because you always ask for turkey dinosaurs and chips. Or pizza!'

'Oh, not anymore. When we go home I want toast and scones every night and be posh.'

'Hmm, I think you'll soon get fed up of that. Come on, sweetie. It's really late. You need to put your pyjamas on and get some sleep.'

Jude looked at her with a serious expression on his face. 'We'll be safe now, Mum, won't we?'

'Jude, darling . . . ' She went and sat on the bed next to him. 'We were safe before. We only came here because our house was surrounded by reporters. It's not because anyone is after us.'

Jude shook his head vigorously. 'No, Tony knows we're in danger, that's why he brought us here.'

'Jude, don't get any romantic notions about Tony. From the looks of things, he has his own problems. We can only stay here for a night or two, and then we have to either go home or find somewhere else to stay. We can't put upon him or his parents any longer than that.'

'Oh no, Mum, I don't think Tony will let us leave. He's going to go and investigate and I know he won't give up until he's found the killer.'

Patty did not want to upset her son by telling him that Tony had no intentions of finding Jason's killer. Everything had happened too smoothly, including the reporters turning up and his sudden ability to conjure up a helicopter to take them to safety.

She was convinced that he had brought her to Fazeby Hall to keep an eye on her because he suspected her of murder.

10

By the following morning, Patty had talked herself out of that ridiculous assumption. In the daylight it seemed a ludicrous idea. It helped her to get over it because Diana was so utterly charming and natural at breakfast.

Whatever the duchess's real feelings about Patty and Jude, she was nothing other than welcoming. 'Do help yourself to breakfast,' she said to them both. 'Harry and Tony were up talking late last night, so I doubt they'll be down for a while yet.'

'Are they friends again?' asked Jude.

'Jude!' Patty glared at him. 'I've told you it's none of our business. Come and get some breakfast.' She led him to a side table which was laid out with bacon, scrambled eggs, devilled kidneys and other goodies.

'Just like *Downton*,' Jude whispered gleefully.

'I love watching *Downton Abbey* too,' said Diana. 'I suppose we do live a bit that way, though I hope we're a little more in touch with the real world.'

Patty and Jude filled their plates with food and sat down. Stephens was on hand to pour out coffee for Patty and juice for Jude.

'Are you feeling better, Jude?' asked Diana. 'Tony mentioned that you weren't very well last night.'

'I'm alright,' said Jude, becoming glum.

'I'm sorry if I wasn't supposed to know,' said Diana.

'It's alright,' said Patty. 'Jude just gets a bit upset about it.'

'I thought I'd stopped having fits,' he said. 'The doctor said I should grow out of them.'

'Well, you have had a lot going on lately,' Diana said soothingly. 'I'm not surprised it made you unwell. Personally I think you've been very brave for your mum.'

'So do I,' said Patty, blessing Diana for allowing Jude a bit of pride.

'My other son, Will, had convulsions when he was little,' Diana explained. 'He grew out of them too.'

'Where is Will now?' asked Jude.

'He died about ten years ago, dear.'

'Oh. I'm really sorry to hear that, Duchess.'

'He was the Marquis of Fazeby,' said Diana, in a faraway voice, as if she were remembering. 'And when he died, the title passed to Anthony, only he didn't want it. You probably know about him and Will falling out.'

'Actually no,' said Patty. 'Believe it or not, last night was only the second time I'd met Tony . . . Anthony. He just happened to be at our house when the press arrived. He's investigating on behalf of the insurance company and he had come around to ask me questions.'

Diana's eyes widened in surprise. 'Really? I thought . . . Well, it doesn't matter what I thought.'

'Why did they fall out?' asked Jude.

Patty was half embarrassed that he had asked, and half glad because she would like to know the answer. There was a lot to be said for being only ten years old and being able to say what you wanted.

'Why do brothers who have been close all their lives ever fall out?' asked Diana, sadly. 'It was over a girl. It was a young actress whom Anthony met. Unfortunately, when she realised that Will was the heir to Fazeby and that she could be a duchess one day, she switched her affections to him.'

'That is unfortunate,' said Patty.

'Yes. That young lady caused a lot of problems in this family. As soon as Will was dead, she came sniffing around Anthony again. He was not very kind to her, as I remember, but perhaps she did not deserve kindness.'

'So is that why Tony went to America?' asked Patty. 'Because he was heartbroken?'

'That, and because he did not want to be the heir to the dukedom. He was so angry at the time.' Diana shook her head slowly, as if trying to eradicate the memory. 'He said he didn't want Will's cast-offs, and that included the girl and the title.'

'Isn't it a bit early in the morning for my life story, Mum? I'm sure Patty is not interested in the soap opera that is the Fazeby family, anyway.'

Patty turned her head. She had not heard Tony enter the room because she had been so engrossed in Diana's story of the two brothers. His voice was harsh and bitter.

'Don't be unkind to your mother,' chided Patty. 'She is not to blame for what happened.'

'No, I'm aware of that, thank you,' said Tony. He took a deep breath and then went to kiss his mother on her forehead. 'I'm sorry. I just didn't expect to be faced with the past quite so quickly.'

'I'm sorry too,' said Diana gently. 'I have no wish to hurt you, my darling. Did you have a good talk with your father?'

Tony had gone to fill up his plate with food. 'Not really. We were only a few minutes behind you.'

'Oh, I thought you were up late, because your father didn't come to bed till the early hours.'

'He might have been up late, but I wasn't.'

And that seemed to be all there was to say on that subject. Patty had a mental image of the two men who looked so much alike being oceans apart when it came to the dukedom. Although she had criticised Tony for being harsh with his mother, she could not help feeling sorry for him. To lose his girl to his brother, and then to for his brother to die before they could make things up, must have been very hard on him.

'I need to go out this morning,' said Tony, sitting down with his breakfast. The ever-reliable Stephens appeared out of nowhere to pour his coffee. 'Thank you, Stephens.' He glanced across at Patty. 'Will you and Jude be alright hanging around here today?'

'Yes, of course, if your mother and father don't mind.'

'We don't,' said Diana.

'I'll try and sort us out a place to stay,' said Patty.

'You can stay here,' said Tony.

'Not indefinitely,' said Patty. 'We're very grateful for your hospitality, Diana, but we don't want to put on you for any longer than necessary.'

'It's no bother. I must say it's nice to have a child in the house again,' Diana said. 'And I did promise to show Jude around! Would you like to see the musket holes in the turret, Jude?'

'Not half,' said Jude, his eyes like saucers.

'Then I'll show you after breakfast.'

'I'm ready now,' said Jude.

'No you're not,' said Patty, firmly. 'You'll finish what's on your plate and drink your juice first.'

'Yes, Mum,' Jude droned. But he was a good boy and did as he was told. Ten minutes later he wiped his mouth with a napkin and said to Diana, 'I'm ready when you are, Duchess.'

'Well we'll start by agreeing that you can call me Aunt Diana,' said the duchess with her warm smile.

'Yes, Aunt Diana.'

'Come along then.'

They stood up to leave. When Jude reached the door, he turned back to Tony. 'You're going to investigate today, aren't you?'

Patty noticed a shadow cross Tony's eyes. 'Yeah, of course, mate, just like we said.'

She waited until Jude and Diana were out of the room before she said, 'Please don't lie to my son, Tony. I'll forgive most things, but not that.'

'I'm not lying. I have a few avenues I want to explore.'

'And how many of those avenues have to do with Jason, Andy and Olivia being murdered?'

The shadow crossed his eyes again. 'I won't let Jude down,' he said, looking down at his plate sheepishly.

'You'd better not,' she said, bitterly. 'Because he's the only reason I might ever want to kill.'

She had been speaking metaphorically and was probably being overdramatic — she was in that sort of mood — but the look of alarm in Tony's eyes made her wish she had not spoken out so passionately.

It was a sunny afternoon in London when Tony got out of the tube at Regent's Park station, so he walked the rest of the way to Harley Street. As he walked, he thought about how hard Patty's eyes had become when she said that Jude was the only reason she might kill.

Everything about her confused him. He knew he was attracted to her. It was something he could not deny, even if he wanted to. But he did not trust her. That was probably because of his previous experience with an actress, but also because he knew Patty was hiding something about Jason Carter. He hoped to have his suspicions confirmed in Harley Street. He walked along the discreet London villas that housed some of the most expensive physicians in the world, until he found the one he wanted. A brass nameplate said that it was the surgery of Doctor Natalie Leopardi. It also named her associates.

'I have an appointment with Doctor Leopardi at two,' he told the receptionist in the hushed waiting area. As he waited, at least two Arab princes and one young woman that he was sure he had seen in the company of a minor royal came out of the doors leading into the individual offices and left by the front door.

'The doctor will see you now,' said the receptionist. 'It's along the hallway — the very last door.'

Tony nodded his thanks and followed the directions. His feet almost got lost in the expensive carpeting. Everything about the building screamed money. Doctor Leopardi was obviously doing well for herself.

She opened the door and waited for him. He had expected a much older woman, but Natalie Leopardi was a stunner, with long natural blonde hair. She stood aside to let him in, and he introduced himself.

'Please come in and sit down, Mr Marcus.' She gestured to a plush armchair near to the window. No sitting on hard plastic seats in this surgery. 'Can I get you anything to drink?'

'No, thank you.' Tony sunk into the chair and wondered if he would be able to get out of it again. Doctor Leopardi sat in the opposite chair.

'How may I help you?'

'I gather that you're an expert on epilepsy?'

'That is one of my areas of interest, yes,' she replied. 'Do you have epilepsy?'

'No, I'm sorry, I probably shouldn't be here under false pretences.' Tony took out his identification. 'I am an investigator with Cassell and Keep. They investigate insurance fraud. I wanted to ask you about epilepsy because it might be relevant to a case that I'm working on.'

'Very well.' The doctor did not look too pleased. She glanced at her watch. 'I really can't give you much time. I do have patients with genuine problems.' Her voice was reproachful.

'Of course, I understand. My main question is whether epilepsy is hereditary.'

'You could have found that out on the internet, Mr Marcus.' She raised an eyebrow.

'And half the information would have been incorrect or skewed by the opinion of the blogger who wrote it. Please humour me, Doctor Leopardi. Is it hereditary?'

'It can be. It depends on the type of epilepsy.'

'Hmm, I'm not really sure,' said Tony, kicking himself for not asking Patty more about Jude's condition. He had not wanted her to know that he was on the right track. 'The person who has it is a child and all I know is that his mother has been told he might grow out of it by the time he's fifteen.'

'Is he on medication?'

'No, he isn't.'

'It sounds very much like Benign Rolandic Epilepsy. If it is, the mother is correct — the child should grow out of it. As to it being hereditary, then it is possible that he inherited it from one of his parents.'

'But how can the child have a different type of epilepsy to the parent who has it?'

'It's a very complex condition. It's fairer to say that in most cases children grow out of epilepsy, but some don't. It's possible the parent did not. Without knowing anything more about the child or the parent, I could not tell you.'

'Which parent is he most likely to inherit it from?'

'It could be either parent, but with epilepsy there's more chance of the father passing on the affliction. It's a very small margin, though, so I wouldn't like to say for certain that was the case.'

'Yes, that's what I thought,' said Tony.

And it was what he had found out on the internet. 'I only have one more question for you, Doctor Leopardi. Am I right in thinking that you treated the late Jason Carter?'

At that Doctor Leopardi's face froze. Tony saw realisation dawn, and it occurred to him for the first time that she was probably Jude's doctor too. 'I am afraid I couldn't tell you who I treat in this surgery. You do understand patient confidentiality?'

'Yes, of course.' Tony smiled understandingly. At least she had not denied knowing Jason Carter. 'But as he's dead . . . '

'If there is a legal reason to know whether or not I treated Jason Carter, then I am sure that you could get a subpoena requesting a look at my records, Mr Marcus. But as you don't seem to have come prepared, I can neither confirm nor deny that he was a patient of mine.'

Tony stood up. He did not really need any more. Natalie Leopardi's response to Jason Carter's name had told him all he needed to know. He held out his hand. 'Thank you for your time.'

She stood up and took his hand, then led him to the door. 'May I ask why you need to know all this?' she asked.

'If Mr Carter was epileptic, he hid the fact on his insurance form.'

'I see. And so your job is to do his son out of his inheritance.'

'I don't quite see it like that,' said Tony, feeling a prickle of annoyance on the back of his neck. He was getting fed up with people making him feel guilty for doing his job. 'I see it as upholding the law.'

'You were quite happy to bend it a few minutes ago to find out what you wanted to know.'

'*Touché*,' he said. But he was not going to be chased off just yet. There was one more link in the chain. 'By the way, Julius Caesar was epileptic, wasn't he?'

'I believe so, but they called it the

'falling down sickness' then,' said Doctor Leopardi.

'From what I read,' said Tony, 'Caesar didn't like people knowing about it.'

'People treated epilepsy differently in those days. Some mistook it for possession by demons. In fact, there are still some prejudices around the illness nowadays.'

'Are you saying that's why Jason Carter kept it a secret, Doctor Leopardi?'

'I wouldn't know if he did or not, Mr Marcus,' she replied coldly.

As he left her office, he saw her pick up a mobile phone from her desk and dial a number. He wished he could hang around to see who she spoke to, but she walked forward and gave the door a kick with her foot. With the big heavy door shut, the room appeared to be soundproof.

It did not matter. As far as Tony was concerned he had found out all he needed to know. Jude had possibly inherited epilepsy from his father. Patty probably knew that but she had kept it quiet. Doctor Leopardi had touched a raw nerve with Tony. If he reported this to his superiors, then it would probably negate Jason Carter's insurance. That would prevent Jude being paid out for his father's death.

As he walked back to the tube, he told himself that it did not matter. Patty had been adamant that she could support her son, and Jason Carter had left other money and property to the tune of several million pounds. It did beg the question of why Patty kept Jason's epilepsy a secret. Could it be that she wanted even more money for her son?

He needed a drink. Stepping out of the office on Harley Street, he turned and went in search of the nearest pub.

11

'Did you find anything out, Tony?' Jude asked anxiously as they all sat down to dinner that night.

Patty glared at Tony across the table, daring him to tell a lie. She had received a call from Natalie Leopardi as Tony was leaving the Harley Street office, so she knew exactly where he had been and what he thought he knew.

'Not today,' Tony said. 'I had a meeting to do with work and it . . . er . . . ran on longer than I thought.' From what Patty had heard it had been a very short interview, with Doctor Leopardi giving him short shrift. But the smell of alcohol on Tony's breath when he returned home suggested he had spent some time in the pub afterwards.

'I found out loads,' Jude said. 'I would have found out more, only Mum took the laptop off me.'

'I'm not sure that some of the sites you were looking at were suitable for a ten-year-old boy,' said Patty. 'In fact, I know they weren't.'

'Olivia used to be a pole dancer,' said Jude.

'Really?' Tony grinned. 'I can see why your mum took the laptop from you.'

'She gave it up to go to make-up school,' Jude said, warming to his theme, 'but she might have had johns then who wanted her dead.'

'Jude!' Patty looked across at the duke and duchess. Thankfully they only looked amused by Jude's enthusiasm. 'Just because she was a pole dancer doesn't mean she had . . . ' Patty almost choked on the next word. ' . . . clients. And where on earth did you hear the term 'johns'?'

Jude rolled his eyes. 'Honestly Mum, I'm not a baby. The other boys at school tell me stuff.'

'Then it's time to change schools I think,' said Patty, horrified about what her son might be hearing.

'Boys will talk about such things,' said the duke, kindly. 'It's probably healthier that they do. And I must say it's very encouraging that Jude will tell you all about it. Some sons don't tell their parents anything.' He cast a regretful look at his own son.

'Do you think so?' asked Patty. 'Yes, I suppose it is good that he talks about it to me.' She smiled at her son. 'But I don't want you looking at anymore pole dancing sites, okay? Besides, whatever Olivia did before, she worked hard to become a make-up artist, and she deserves respect for that. It isn't kind to think of her in terms of . . . johns and whatever she did to pay the bills whilst pole dancing.' It was important to Patty that Jude grow up with a healthy respect for women, regardless of how they started out in life. She only prayed he would take on board what she had said.

'Okay. What else did I have to tell Tony? Oh yes, Andy Paxton was busted for dealing drugs about fifteen years

139

ago, when he was working as a taxi driver. He did five years in prison. Maybe he owed money to a drugs lord.'

'Oh my God,' said Patty, putting her head in her hands, not knowing whether to laugh or cry. 'And I thought the pole dancing was bad enough. Anyway, darling,' she said, trying to compose herself, 'those two things don't link the deaths, do they? Your father hadn't been a pole dancer or a drug dealer as far as I'm aware.'

'Would you admit it if he had?' said Tony, in pointed tones.

Patty looked up sharply. 'I don't think it would be a suitable conversation to have in front of my son, do you?'

'Jude seems able to cope with anything.'

'Well as you found out last night, he isn't.'

'Anthony,' said Diana, 'you're being very rude to our guests. Guests that you invited, I might add. I'm sure that Patty is the best person to decide what her son needs to hear about his father.'

All the time they were speaking, Jude was watching Patty avidly, as if wondering if she had kept secrets from him. 'Your father was a good man,' she said to him. 'And he loved you very much. That's all you ever need to know about him.'

'I know, Mum, but if we're to find out who killed Daddy, then we might need to know some of the bad stuff. That's what the crime books say. You have to know about the victims.'

'There wasn't any 'bad stuff', my angel. Daddy liked to have pretty women around him, yes, but that doesn't make him an evil person. I can assure you that he did not do drugs, or even drink alcohol.'

'Rather strange for a hell-raiser,' said Tony under his breath.

Patty put her napkin down. 'I think Jude and I have outstayed our welcome,' she said. 'Your Grace, thank you for your hospitality . . . '

'I'm sorry,' said Tony. 'I shouldn't have said that. Please don't go, Patty.

I've had a long day and I'm very tired. I didn't mean to upset either of you. Jude, it's unforgivable of me to talk about your dad like that. I'm really sorry. I hope we're still friends.'

'Yes, of course,' said Jude, but he sounded doubtful.

An hour later, Patty put Jude to bed. 'I don't think Tony likes us anymore,' he said sadly.

'I'm sure he likes you, darling,' she said, ruffling his hair and tucking him under the covers. 'It's as I said, we've perhaps outstayed our welcome. Sometimes people think they want to help, but then regret it. I think that's what's happened with Tony. We'll go somewhere else tomorrow.'

'I'd like to go home. It's very nice here, and I loved the duchess telling me all about the Civil War, and showing me the musket holes in the battlements, but I miss my own room.'

'Then we'll go home. We'll find some way of avoiding the reporters.'

Jude nodded sadly in agreement.

'Tony's not going to find Daddy's killer, is he?'

'No, darling, I don't think he is. That's why I didn't want you building your hopes up.'

Jude held out his hand to her. 'We'll find who it was, won't we, Mum?'

Patty nodded, coming to a decision in that moment. They did not need Tony. 'Yes, darling, we will.' She kissed his head. 'But no more dubious websites!'

'A detective sometimes has to plumb the murky depths,' said Jude in such a way that it made Patty burst out laughing.

'Not ten-year-old detectives! You let me plumb the murky depths, alright?'

'But I have to protect you, Mum, now that Dad's not here and Tony doesn't want to do it.' He paused to think for a moment. 'I wonder if Matt would do it. He looks pretty tough and even though he's not a real gladiator, he had to do all the training. I read about it online. He broke his arm once during filming.'

Patty made a mental note to monitor Jude's Internet browsing for a while. 'I'll have you know that I don't need a man to take care of me. Well, except you, and it's not really your job to look after me, my darling. It's my job to look after you.'

'We have to take care of each other, mum. That's what dad would have wanted.'

★   ★   ★

'Anthony, I'd like to speak to you in the study, please.' Harry got up from the table. He went and kissed his wife on the cheek. 'You don't mind, do you, darling? I'll join you in the drawing room later.'

'Not at all. It's about time you two had a proper talk, instead of skulking around each other all the time.'

Tony picked up his glass of port and took it with him. He figured he was going to need it.

Harry shut the library door. 'Would

you mind telling me what the hell is going on here?' he asked.

'What do you mean?' The two men stood almost toe-to-toe, neither willing to back down.

'You bring that charming woman and that wonderful boy into this house and then proceed to make them feel unwelcome.'

'I apologised.'

'It wasn't enough, Anthony! When you brought them here, you made them my guests, and I won't have my guests treated in that way. All those snide remarks at that poor woman's expense. And in front of her son. What were you thinking?'

'Oh that's rich coming from you,' said Tony. 'The master of snide remarks and all about how I'm failing in my duty as your son.'

'You've never failed me as a son, Anthony. But you have abandoned Fazeby Hall.'

'What does it matter?' asked Tony. 'Fazeby was never meant to be mine anyway. It was supposed to be Will's. I always was the second-best son.'

'No, not that,' said Harry. 'Never that, whatever you might think. Yes, Fazeby was meant for William as the eldest son, but he's not here now. You are, and I want you to love this place as much as I do. I want you to care what happens to it. Is that too much to ask?'

'How do you think I feel, knowing that my brother was always the one who would have everything? He even took my girlfriend! And now I'm supposed to accept his leavings?'

'Will you listen to yourself, Anthony? Young Jude is more mature that you are. This isn't about taking Will's leavings, as you put it. I don't blame you for not wanting that girl. She was a gold digger, pure and simple. Even Will realised that in the end.'

'When did he realise it?' Tony took a step back. The tension had gone out of the situation.

'Before he went away that last time. He'd broken up with her, partly out of guilt for betraying you and partly because he opened his eyes to what she really was.'

'I didn't know that.' He remembered ignoring messages from his brother, because he was still angry with him. Was that why Will had tried to get in touch with him?

'He wanted to make things up with you, and he told me he was going to call in and see you when he returned from his trip.'

'Why didn't you tell me?'

'What chance did I get? The moment his funeral was over, you were off to America.'

'They have telephones, even in America.'

'Alright,' Harry sighed. 'I was angry with you for going. So I decided it didn't matter what Will was going to say to you. I'm sorry. What I want to know is, whether you're treating Patty the way you are because of that other girl.'

'She's an actress too, and an even better one,' Tony said, bitterly.

'What do you mean?'

'She's lying to me, dad.'

'Do you think she killed her ex-husband?'

'I don't know about that, but she's certainly keeping secrets from me. Jason Carter was epileptic, and it's something he should have told the insurers, but he didn't. I think she knows but is not telling for some reason.'

'Why don't you ask her outright?'

'I have . . . sort of.'

'Hmm, that's what I thought.'

'What does that mean?'

'It's just like with Will and that girl. You were determined back then to wait until he was honest with you, instead of asking him outright.'

'He was seeing her. What was there to be honest about?'

'If you'd talked about it with him, instead of being so furious with him, it might have shamed him into giving her up sooner. But you became angry, and then he became angry that you were angry with him. And in the middle there was your mother and I, hurting because the sons we both adored weren't talking to each other. That girl wasn't worth tearing this family apart for, Anthony.'

'Maybe not, but I didn't think that way at the time. I thought I loved her, Dad.'

Harry sighed, his eyes becoming sympathetic. 'I know, son. And I know Will hurt you. But in the end he was hurt too. You need to sort things out with Patty. Don't let this one thing about Jason Carter come between you.'

'What do you mean, come between us? We're not lovers, dad.'

'No, of course not.' Harry's lips curled. 'You bring waifs and strays back here all the time.'

'She was in trouble, and so was Jude, so I thought I'd help, that's all.'

'Hmm,' said Harry, smiling secretively.

Tony ran his hands through his hair. 'Look, Dad, I'm never going to be the Marquis of Fazeby.'

'You already have that title, Anthony, whether you like it or not.'

'No — what I mean is, I'm not going

to take the estate. I'm not cut out for the life you live. But maybe we can come up with some way between us to save it. I can promise you that I won't sell it off in little pieces. Is that enough?'

'I suppose it will have to be for now.'

★ ★ ★

Tony left his father in the library and went to the hallway. Patty was coming down the stairs, looking uncertain.

'I think my mother is in the drawing room,' he said.

'Oh, right, thank you. I only came down to say a proper goodnight.'

'It's only nine o'clock, Patty.'

'I know, but . . . Jude and I will be leaving in the morning, so I didn't want to be rude.'

'You don't have to leave. I am sorry about my behaviour earlier. If it makes you feel any better, my dad has just chewed me up about it.'

'And yet you look more relaxed.'

'Yeah, I think we sorted out some

other things too.'

'Good, I'm glad. I'll go and say goodnight to your mum.' By that time, Patty had reached the bottom of the stairs.

'Patty, would it be too difficult for you to be honest with me?'

'Honest about what?'

'About Jason's epilepsy.'

'Oh, that. Yes, alright, Jason was epileptic. There you have it. Now you can go and tell your bosses and you don't need to worry about me and Jude anymore.'

'Does the money mean that much to you?'

She turned on him, her eyes flashing. 'I told you I don't need the money.'

'So why keep it a big secret?'

She breathed out, taking a long time before answering. 'I kept it a secret because Jason asked me to.'

'I don't understand. Why did he keep it a secret? For the insurance?'

'No!' She flushed angrily. 'He was ashamed of his condition, mainly because his parents had been ashamed. They saw it as some sort of curse on the family and treated him that way all his life. He would rather people think that his fits of shaking were to do with alcoholism than epilepsy, hence his reputation as a hell-raiser. Oh don't get me wrong, Jason could raise hell when he wanted, but he was no alcoholic or drug addict. When he told me he was epileptic, he made me promise that I would never tell. A promise might not mean much to you,' she said pointedly. 'But it meant everything to me.'

Tony wanted to believe she was telling the truth. Everything she had said seemed plausible enough, but something irked him about it. If he were honest, he would have recognised it as jealousy. He was envious that Jason Carter, a man who could not even remain faithful to the most beautiful woman in the world, could still inspire such trust. That jealousy made Tony behave more harshly than he really intended.

'And you don't think that by hiding

Jude away the way you do that you're making him just as ashamed of his epilepsy? I mean, that's the real reason you didn't want anyone to know, wasn't it? So no one would know that the perfect actress had given birth to a child who was less than perfect?' If he had set out to hurt her, it appeared to work. Her eyes took on a wounded, agonised look. It swiftly changed to anger.

'How dare you?' she stormed, curling her hand into a fist. For a moment he thought she was going to slap him, but she put her hand resolutely by her side. 'How dare you accuse me of being ashamed of my boy? He is my proudest achievement. If I keep him out of the spotlight it's to protect him and because I want him to have a normal life. He is not just a fashion accessory to be rolled out for premieres. Can you imagine what his life would be like? Especially if they did find out he's epileptic. The news-papers and magazines would be full of stories about him, just to sell a few extra copies. And even then people will say

I'm only talking about it to get publicity for my films, when it's really the papers feeding the ghoulish demands of the public. I will not have my son subjected to that. I want him to know that he is important to me in his own right, and not because of any extra column inches he can get me.'

'Well I hope he knows that,' said Tony, still angry about Jason. He saw Patty swallow hard, as tears filled her eyes. 'Because from where I'm standing it looks as if you're just hiding him away. First his father teaches him to be ashamed of his condition, and now you do.'

'We clearly have outstayed our welcome,' she said in a low, agonised voice. 'In fact I wonder why you invited us here at all, unless it was with the sole intention of humiliating me. Please give your mother my regrets and tell her I've gone to bed with a headache. We'll leave first thing in the morning.'

'Patty . . . ' Oh you idiot, he said to himself, take it all back. Take it all back quickly. Tell her you're sorry. Jealousy had cost him his brother and now it was going to cost him Patty, and he did not want her to go. It was too late. She was already halfway up the stairs, and even as she was walking further into the house, and would not leave until the next morning, he knew that he was losing her. She turned back, eying him coldly, looking imperious and every bit the queen of all she surveyed. He was reminded of the original film of *Cleopatra* when the Egyptian queen forced Marc Antony to bow to her. In his anger, he felt that Patty was asking the same of him. Maybe not in physical terms, but in expecting him to leave things be where Jason's epilepsy was concerned. But her next words surprised him.

'Tell your bosses whatever you need to tell them,' Patty said. 'I really could not care less about the money. But I'd better not find a ton of reporters outside my house, wanting to know every detail of my son's condition. I will not have him used to get column inches!'

'You know I love you, don't you?' Patty said, stroking Jude's hair a short time later. He lay dozing in bed in the small room next to hers, and she did not really want to disturb him, but she had been so het up by Tony's words that she needed to see her son.

'I know, Mum.'

'And you know I'm very proud of you, don't you?'

'What's wrong, Mum? Why are you crying?' Jude sat up, and Patty immediately felt guilty. She should not be involving him in her angst. He had been through too much already.

'It's just, I don't want you to think the reason I keep you out of the limelight is because I'm ashamed of you. Or your condition.'

'Dad was ashamed of it though, wasn't he?'

'Not of you, darling! No, never.'

'He was ashamed of having epilepsy.'

'Yes, he was, but that was because of

how his parents brought him up. They were ashamed of it, so he grew up thinking it was something he should hide. I didn't realise till Tony said it that it might seem as if I'm hiding you away for the same reason. I'm not, my angel. I just want you to have a proper childhood away from all the cameras.'

'I know, Mum. You wait till I see Tony.' Jude's small hands curled into fists just as his mother's had a few minutes earlier. It was touching and pathetic all at once. 'I don't really like him much anymore.'

'He's just been doing his job, Jude. The one he's paid to do. That's why I didn't want you to get your hopes up about him helping us.'

'But why did he bring us here if he didn't want to help us?'

'I think to keep an eye on me.'

'Because he thinks you killed Dad? But that's not his job either. So it doesn't make sense.'

'No, it doesn't. Unless he's just curious, or he wants a big case to solve to get famous. Never mind that now. I'm sorry I disturbed you.' Patty pulled the covers up over Jude's shoulders. 'I just needed to see you, that's all.' She kissed his head. 'Try not to worry about me or Tony or anything else. We'll go home tomorrow and face whatever comes.'

12

Early the next morning, and after a sleepless night, Tony found Jude and his father fishing by the lake.

'Morning Dad. Morning Jude,' he said. His father nodded and smiled in his usual reserved manner. Things were less strained between them, but there were still some miles to go before they saw eye to eye. Jude stared resolutely at the lake.

'Are the fish biting, Jude?' No reply.

'No, they're a bit quiet this morning,' said Harry. 'It's a pity, as Jude wanted some trout to take home with him, didn't you lad?'

Jude nodded as if to be polite to Harry, but still didn't speak.

'So you're going home, are you, Jude? We'll miss you, won't we, Dad?'

'Yes. It's been good to have the lad around. It reminds me of when you and

159

Will were youngsters. Do you remember? Not that you caught many fish. You'd spend most of your time arguing and frightening the fish away.'

'I refuse to believe we were that bad,' said Tony with mock cheerfulness. Jude's silence and refusal to look at him started to bother him. 'What do you think, Jude?'

'I dunno. I wasn't here.'

'No, that's true. Hey, maybe we can persuade your mum to let you stay a bit longer. There's no rush for you to get back.'

'I want to go home,' said Jude.

'I thought you liked it here. Me and Dad were going to look at some cottages that want renovating. We thought you'd like to tag along.'

Harry turned around and stared at Tony in surprise. 'You said you weren't bothered about the estate,' he said.

'Well, I am. And I thought Jude would like to see the village. It was designed by my great-great grandfather, and the cottages have all sorts of battlements and turrets on them, like mini castles. No two cottages are the same. Isn't that right, Dad?'

'Yes, that's right. What do you say, Jude? Do you want to come with us?'

Tony guessed rightly that his father would clutch at any straw to get his only surviving son interested in the estate.

Jude threw his line down. 'No!' He turned on Tony. 'I'm going home, right? I want to go home. I don't want to stay here with you, because you only pretended to be our friend when you're not really.' After his initial rant he looked uncertainly at Harry. 'I'm very sorry, Duke. I don't mean to be rude to you. I would have liked to see the cottages with turrets and battlements, but . . . ' His voice died away and he started to tremble.

'Jude, it's alright, mate,' said Tony, holding out his hand. If Jude had a fit, he would not have a clue how to deal with it. He remembered how calm Patty had seemed when Jude had his previous fit, but he guessed she had to be. It was no good her panicking. He began to realise just how much emotional effort she devoted to her son. 'It's alright.'

'I'm not your mate and you're not mine. I hate you!'

'Jude . . . ' Patty's husky tones filled the morning air. Tony had not heard her approach. 'Jude, everything will be alright, darling. We'll go home and we'll be okay again, I promise.'

Jude ran to his mother's arms. She turned and led him back to the house.

'Patty, do you need any help?'

She looked back over her shoulder. 'No, you've done quite enough for one morning.'

Tony slumped down onto the ground next to his father. The dew from the grass immediately soaked through his jeans, but he did not care.

'Why on earth did you bring them?' asked Harry, looking at his son with kind eyes. The kindness hurt more than if his father had been judging him badly. 'Surely it wasn't just so you could hurt them.'

'I wanted to protect her and be with her. It didn't even matter what she'd done or hadn't done. I just wanted to keep her close.' It was the first time Tony had admitted that to himself, let alone to anyone else.

'So you use her son to get close to her, and you use me and the promise of a trip to the village to get close to her son. Have you ever done anything that wasn't for yourself, Anthony?'

Tony grimaced as the words struck home. 'I don't . . . I mean . . . Dad, that wasn't why I said I'd come to the village.'

'Wasn't it? So now that Jude is going home, are you still going to come with me?'

'I don't know.' Tony sighed. 'I have stuff to do. Work and . . . '

'Yes, of course you do. Well, some other time maybe.'

Tony could hardly bear to see the disappointment in his father's eyes. It was even worse to see himself reflected back in them. He had not thought of himself as a selfish man, yet when he looked back, everything he had done since his brother died had been an act of selfishness. He left his mother and father grieving alone at home, and let his father down about taking over the titles and lands of Fazeby. He had buried himself thousands of miles away in America, never contacting them, too busy building up his career.

When he had joined the police force, and then gone on to be an investigator, it was intended as a way of bringing justice to an unjust world. He had dreams and ideals back then. And what had those dreams and ideals come to? Finding out people's secrets so he could deprive them of their insurance money. And worse still, depriving a grief-stricken young boy with epilepsy of the money his father would have wanted him to have.

Tony could not lie to his bosses about Jason Carter's condition. He had to do the job he was paid to do. His honour demanded it. But whether he wanted to be paid to do that job in the future was another matter.

'I'm going to lose them, Dad,' he said, as his newfound self-awareness crushed him. 'Just like I lost you and Mum.'

'You didn't lose us, son,' said Harry. 'You just mislaid us for a while.' His father smiled sadly. 'We were always here, waiting for you to come back. And even if you're only here to impress that young lady and her son, we'll take anything we can get to have our son back in our lives.'

'I don't deserve you both. I don't deserve her. But I'm going to make it up to you all, Dad. I've broken my promise to Jude, but I'm going to make good on it, no matter what happens afterwards.'

'Good.'

'But first let's go and look at those cottages, hey?'

Harry smiled, widely this time. 'Yes, let's. But first go and make your peace with Patty. Even if she leaves today, we want her to know she can always come back.'

Tony nodded and patted his dad on the shoulder. He would have given his father a hug, but he was not sure how Harry would take it. His father was not a tactile man. He just hoped that he would feel the love that was in his heart.

Patty was packing her clothes when Tony found her.

'Is Jude alright?' he asked.

'Yes, he's fine. He's packing in his room.'

'I'll go and see him.'

'No, please don't, Tony. You've upset him enough.'

'I just want to say I'm sorry. To both of you. I wish you weren't leaving.'

'I have to leave anyway. I'm going back to work on Monday.'

'To the film?'

'Yes, my agent has been on the phone. The producers are insisting that the filming go ahead, and if I don't attend, it will cost me dearly.'

'But people are dying . . . '

'You don't have to tell me that.' She glared at him.

'You can't go back, Patty. Jude will worry his little self sick about you. Let them find the killer first. I'm sure any good lawyer will argue that you can't put your life at risk.'

'Well thank you for your sudden concern for my son's welfare, and for mine, but we'll manage.'

'I am concerned about you. Why do you think I brought you here?'

'To keep an eye on me? Or to find out the secret of Jason's epilepsy? Both are possible.'

'No. I brought you and Jude here to protect you both. Because I . . . ' He wondered what she would say if he told her that he loved her. She might laugh at him, as the other actress had laughed when he begged her not to leave him for his brother. Part of him doubted that Patty was that cruel, but his fear won the day. 'I care about you both.'

'Why? You'd known us less than an hour in total when you brought us here.'

'So why did you come?'

She faltered and looked down at her suitcase. 'I don't know. I was panicked, I suppose, by all the reporters outside. My home had never been violated by the press like that before. I had nowhere else to go.' She took a deep breath. 'I am grateful, Tony. I don't want you to think I'm not. Jude is too, despite what he said this morning. He doesn't hate you. In fact I think that he likes you a lot, like . . . ' She stopped and clamped her lips shut, leaving Tony wondering what she was going to say next. Like me? 'Like hero-worship,' she said instead, but he felt sure that was not her original intention. 'I did warn him not to make a hero of you, but it's the glamour, I suppose, of you being a private investigator. He thinks it's like in the films.' She smiled. 'He should know better really, being the son and grandson of actors, but he still has that child-like view of it all. He can overlook the greasepaint and the painted scenery or the blue screen and still see the magic. I sometimes wish I could still see things that way. Experience has a way of showing you the peeling paint and the jerky rolling backdrop of life.'

Tony walked across to her and put his hands on her shoulders. 'Patty?'

She turned her face up to him. 'What?'

'Life can still be magic. We just have to look for it, I suppose.'

'I gave up looking for it a long time ago.'

'You talk like an old woman, when you're what? Twenty-nine? Thirty?'

She grinned up at him. 'You can't expect an actress to admit her age. If I did that, I'd be playing Matt Archer's grandmother in the next film I do.'

The mention of Matt Archer broke the spell. Tony dropped his hands and moved away. 'Yeah, well, I'm sure he'll be glad you're back at work.'

'Yes, he says so.'

'You've spoken to him?'

'Hmm, on the phone about five minutes ago. He's been ordered back to the set too.'

'I see. Well, I'm sure you'll have a nice reunion.'

'Hardly, when my ex-husband and Matt's girlfriend have been murdered.' Patty's voice had become harder. He could tell by her eyes that she was perplexed by the sudden change in mood.

'No, that was a stupid thing for me to say, sorry.' Tony sighed. 'I seem to spend my whole life apologising to people lately. I'd better go and see my father, before I put my foot in it again.'

'I'm glad you and your dad are getting on,' she said, softly.

'Yeah. Me too. Tell Jude I said good-bye, will you?'

'Tony?'

'What?'

'I don't blame you for doing your job. I just want you to know that. If I was angry with you, it wasn't about the money.

It was because I was protecting Jason.'

'Yes, I know. You must have loved him a lot.' Another dagger to Tony's heart.

'I did, once. Mostly I respected him as the father of my child.'

'Jude is a great kid. If he ever forgives me, tell him I said that, will you?'

'I will.'

Tony considered telling her of his plan, but he decided against it. He did not know if he could find out who killed Jason, Andy and Olivia, and he did not want to make any more promises he could not keep.

'If you or Jude ever need me, Patty, you just have to say the word.'

'We'll be fine now, I'm sure.'

That was not what he wanted her to say. He wanted her to tell him that she needed him as much as he needed her. It did not occur to him that it might be her pride talking.

He took one last look at her from the door, afraid that if he let her go, he would never get her back again.

13

The events of the previous weeks had done nothing to humble George Cassius. If anything he was more tyrannical, screaming at film crew and actors alike when they failed to live up to his expectations.

'I will make this film!' He had called them together for what was his idea of a pep talk. 'Regardless of the people trying to stop me and ruin my life.'

'It's hardly your life that's ruined,' Patty muttered. She stood next to Matt, who nodded his agreement.

'That's right, Cassius,' he said. 'You're still alive and three people are dead. So can you try to make this a bit less about you?'

'I don't have to listen to this from a man who made his name showing off his abs in some lousy cable television show! Just remember, Archer, that I can replace you at any time with another hungry young actor.'

'Suits me,' said Matt, but the fight had gone out of him. He glanced at Patty apologetically. She smiled back to show that she understood. No one could afford to make enemies in Hollywood. Not even with a monster like George Cassius.

'It isn't about the big break,' he said to her during a break. They sat in the make-up room, drinking coffee. 'It's about staying long enough to find out who killed Olivia.'

A new make-up artist had been appointed, proving Cassius's claim that he could replace anyone. In the film world there was always an understudy waiting in the wings, whether it was onstage or off. Everyone needed a big break and the buzz around the film, even with Cassius at the helm, meant everyone wanted their name on the credits.

'Do you have any ideas?' asked Patty.

Matt shrugged. 'Not many. I've been looking into that group. You know, the one campaigning against us playing ethnic characters. I wondered if they were behind it.'

'I don't think they're violent, are they?'

'No, I don't think so either, but I can't think of any other person who would want Jason, Andy and Olivia dead. None of them met till this production and they didn't move in the same circles. I did wonder if . . . ' he paused.

'What?'

'It doesn't matter.'

'Go on, Matt,' said Patty. 'What did you wonder?'

'I don't want to upset you, but I wondered if Olivia and Jason had an affair at some time.'

'Yes, that occurred to me too, but as far as I know, they didn't. Not that I knew every one of Jason's lovers. I only got to find out in the papers and gossip magazines, like everyone else.'

'And anyway, that doesn't explain Andy's death, unless . . . ' Matt looked bashful again. It was rather sweet of him to worry about her feelings. That was something Tony Marcus sometimes failed to do. Or maybe Tony got to her for other reasons.

'Unless he was selling Jason and Olivia drugs? I can't speak for Olivia, but Jason was very anti-drugs, despite his reputation.'

'Right, so we're back where we started,' said Matt. 'No one person had a motive to want all three of them dead. Look, maybe we could get together on this. We could go out for dinner and discuss it . . . if you're not too busy.' Patty found his bashfulness around her appealing. She knew he was not like that with other girls. He was considered to be a bit cocky and forthright. He seemed a bit intimidated by her, and she was not quite sure she was comfortable with that. She would have to prove to him she was approachable.

'Yes, we could do that.'

'What about tonight?' he asked. 'If Cassius ever lets us leave this place.'

'Tonight will be great. Mum and Dad

are back from their tour, so they can watch Jude.'

'I thought you had a nanny.'

'I do, but I like to spend the evenings with him if Mum and Dad aren't around. So he always has family with him.'

As they spoke, Jude entered the make-up trailer. 'Hey, Mum. Hey, Matt.'

'Hi, cobber,' said Matt. 'I didn't know you were here.'

'Hello, darling,' said Patty. 'Have you done your lessons?'

'Ye-es.'

'He's studying here now?' asked Matt.

'Yes. After the truth about Jason's epilepsy hit the papers, the media started stalking his school. For the sake of the other children, I've pulled him out and hired a private tutor to come to the studio. Reporters are camped outside our house too.'

'Anyway,' said Jude. 'I can keep an eye on Mum here.'

'You won't mind if I take your mum out for a meal tonight, will you, mate?'

'Nah, that's great. Mum needs to go on a date.'

'It's not a date as such,' said Patty. But looking at Matt, she wondered if that was what he thought. 'We're just going out for dinner.' Patty climbed off the make-up chair and pulled off the pieces of tissue which had been used to protect her elaborate gown. It was one of over a hundred she had worn for the production so far. She longed to be back in jeans and a T-shirt. Maybe Matt would not be so intimidated by her if she dressed more casually. As it was, he only saw her in her Cleopatra garb. It was enough to make anyone frightened of her.

'Brill,' said Jude. 'I knew you two were going to be friends the minute I saw you. Matt won't let us down, will he, Mum?'

'Jude, I . . . ' Patty stopped talking because at that moment Tony appeared in the doorway. Judging by the expression on his face, he had heard everything. 'Hello,' she said. 'What brings you here?'

'I'm still doing some work for the insurance company,' said Tony, his lips set in a thin line.

'Haven't you found out enough about my dad?' said Jude, his own expression sullen.

'Jude, remember your manners,' said Patty.

'Sorry,' said Jude, but he did not really sound it.

'It's not about your dad, Jude,' said Tony. 'And I'm sorry for all the trouble I've caused you.'

Jude did not reply.

'What? So now you're trying to do Olivia's family out of her insurance?' said Matt. 'Or is it Andy's? He had a wife and kids you know, and he didn't earn much as an actor.'

'No, nothing like that,' Tony snapped. His eyes were dark and cloudy. 'I don't have to explain myself to anyone, least of all you, Mr Archer. As I'm clearly interrupting something, I'd better go and get on with my work.'

'It's okay, because Matt is going to help us,' said Jude. 'Aren't you, Matt?' He looked up at Matt as if he were some sort of god. 'Him and Mum are going to work together to find out who killed my dad, Tony and Olivia. They're having dinner tonight to discuss it.'

Patty cast an astounded glance at her son. Had Jude also been listening at the door? She would have to have a word with him about it.

'I hope you have a nice time,' said Tony in icy tones. He looked directly at Patty. She wanted to explain to him that it was not a dinner date. She decided it was none of his business anyway. Why did he have to turn up again now? She had hoped never to see him again. At least during the times she was not wishing she could see him again.

'How are your mum and dad?' she asked, to fill the awkward silence that followed.

'They're very well, thank you. Dad's working on those cottages, and I'm going up to help him at the weekend. I was going to ask . . . ' He glanced at Jude, but the child made a point of not looking back. 'It doesn't matter.'

'They've got cottages with turrets and stuff, Matt,' said Jude, sounding bored. 'It's a bit stupid if you ask me.'

'Jude!' Patty admonished her son. 'I'm sorry, Tony, but Jude seems to have really forgotten his manners today.' She understood that Tony had hurt Jude, and it was the only reason her son reacted the way he did, but she did not want him to behave like a brat, regardless of the provocation. He was just a child and did not understand that there were some things you could never take back. She had to stop him before he got to that point.

'Well I did interrupt his meet-up with his best friend, Matt,' said Tony bitterly. 'I'll be on my way.' He left the make-up trailer. Patty went to the door and watched him walk away, her heart heavy.

'Sorry, Mum,' said Jude.

'I'm not the one you should be

apologising to,' she said, sounding irritated. 'Tony and his parents gave us a place to stay when we needed it, so I think you could be a little more grateful. Really, Jude, I'm disappointed in you. Tony did not promise us anything more than that help, so why you're so unkind to him I don't know.'

'He made you cry,' said Jude.

Patty coughed awkwardly. She did not want Matt to know about that. 'It was an emotional time,' she explained, looking at Matt. 'For all of us.'

'Sure, I understand. You have to treat the guy with respect, mate,' Matt said to Jude. 'If he helped you out and all that. You should apologise the next time you see him.'

'Okay, Matt, I will, if you say I should.'

Patty rolled her eyes heavenward, wondering how long it would be before Jude was disappointed in Matt. Her son had a habit of putting people on a pedestal, and it was one from which it was dangerously easy to fall.

181

Tony stood at the doors to the sound stage, taking deep calming breaths. He had no claim on Patty, so it was none of his business if she went out with Matt. Yet the thought of it cut him to shreds. The guy was too handsome for his own good. Tony knew that he was not that bad-looking, but he could not compete with a big strapping Australian with fair hair and tanned skin. It was a real tan too, not out of a bottle. Tony would prefer to think the guy was a fake, but he did not seem to be. He seemed like a good bloke, apart from the fact that he was wooing the woman that Tony was in love with.

'Who are you and what are you doing on my set?' said a voice behind him. Tony turned to see George Cassius glaring at him.

'I'm Tony Marcus and I've been sent here by Cassell and Keep on behalf of the insurance company.' It was only half a lie. He had told his bosses that he had

182

some loose ends to tie up, and that would mean spending a bit of time on the set. He flashed his studio pass.

'I know what you're up to, and it's like I told the crew this morning, I'm not going to be bullied out of this job.'

'Really?' said Tony. 'And how many people are going to have to die on this set before you stop thinking of yourself and start considering the true cost of this production?'

'Do you know who I am? I am George Cassius. I am the greatest director that ever lived. Never mind Hitchcock. Forget your Spielbergs and Lucases! They just made films for the masses. I make masterpieces.'

'Masterpieces that lose money,' said Tony. 'From what I can make out, unless someone really dies — like that actor in your last movie — people won't pay to see them.'

'I don't expect you to understand art, Mr . . . '

'Marcus.'

'Marcus. I don't expect you to know

about making great films. I will make a great film and it will win Oscars, and then the academy will be sorry they've snubbed me for so long. Now get off my set.'

'No.'

'What?'

'I said no. I have permission to be here and if you try to evict me, I will tell Cassell and Keep and the producers of this film that you are hampering a genuine investigation. Then they will shut you down, and you can wave bye-bye to your Oscars. I'm here to make sure there are no more murders, Mr Cassius, and I intend to do that job.' It was a massive bluff, and one that might be easily disproved if Cassius contacted the right people. Tony rightly guessed that George Cassius was not a man to make insecure telephone calls asking if his production was safe. A flicker in the man's eyes told Tony that his words had hit home.

'You keep out of my way,' said Cassius.

'I will, but first of all I need to speak to you.'

'I don't have time.'

'You will make time, unless you really do want to hamper my investigation.'

'Very well, but not now. I'll speak to you later, after today's filming has finished. Come to my hotel and we'll talk then.'

'Good. Whilst I'm here I'll talk to a few other people. Who is the best person to give me a tour of the studio?'

'Wait a minute.' Cassius turned around. 'Carla, come here.' A fair-haired girl came out of the shadows. 'Look after Mr Marcus here, but keep him out of my way.'

'Yes, Mr Cassius.'

'Thanks, Carla,' said Tony, when Cassius had gone.

'It's Carmen, actually.'

'Oh, sorry. Carmen.'

'I don't expect you to remember. No one ever does. They all take their cue from him. Apart from Ms Carter. She always remembers. She's a nice lady.'

There was something rueful in Carmen's voice. He guessed that as one of the underlings, she got bossed around a lot.

'Yes, that's what I've heard,' said Tony.

'What do you want to see, Mr Marcus?'

'Call me Tony. Maybe we could have a talk first. Where can we grab some coffee around here?'

Carmen took him to the back of the sound studio, where the vending machines, a table full of snacks and a large urn were set up. She deftly made up a pot of fresh coffee and poured it for him. 'Help yourself to a Danish pastry,' she said. 'No one ever eats on set, so most of it gets thrown out.'

'Why don't they eat?'

'You haven't spent much time around actresses, have you, Mr Marcus?' asked Carmen wryly. He wanted to tell her she was wrong, but it was true he had only known one actress socially. In Hollywood he saw them all over the place, but he did not move in the same

186

circles. 'They never eat in public,' Carmen continued. 'They only ever eat in their trailers and then you only have their word for it that they've eaten. If they dare put on a few ounces in the day, the camera is merciless in showing it.'

'Ms Carter seems to have a healthy enough appetite.'

'How do you know?' Carmen frowned. 'Yes, you're right though. She's not as uptight about food as other actresses.'

'You seem to like her a lot.'

'As I said, she's nice and she remembers my name.'

'So you don't think she killed her ex-husband then?'

'I'm not sure, really. I know they suspected her. But from what I could see, her and Mr Carter got on really well.'

'Have you got any idea how the blood might have got onto her dress?'

Carmen shrugged. 'No, I can't think how it got there. Some of the special effects people were mixing blood that day for a big battle scene.'

'But not real blood?'

'No, it was some mixture they use.'

'What about Andy Paxton? How did he die, exactly?'

'They said he drank some poison during his death scene. Real poison, that is. It's some stuff they use in special effects, but I can't remember what it's called.'

'The same poison that killed Olivia, the make-up girl. What did you think of those two? Andy and Olivia?'

'They were alright. He was a bit of a wide boy. He used to be in that teen soap. He played a villain in that — the dad of one of the teenagers — and I don't think he had to act too much. They say he used to deal drugs.'

'Yes, so I hear. Who handled the poison? I mean, the prop poison he was supposed to drink?'

'Well it wouldn't be real poison, of course. It would just be coloured water.'

'Yes, sorry,' said Tony, with a 'How dumb am I?' grin. 'I mean, who handled all that?'

'It could be anyone on this production. Mr Cassius drives the unions mad, because if he screams at someone to go and do something, they do it, even if it isn't their job. He gets into no end of trouble because of it. I can take you to the props department if you want and you can talk to them.'

'Yes, in a while. How long have you been working for Mr Cassius?'

'This is my third film with him.'

'And still he can't get your name right?'

'Everyone says he's a genius,' said Carmen, colouring up. 'So I have to make allowances for him. One day I want to direct my own films, and I'm learning so much from him.'

'How to scream at people,' Tony suggested.

'I hope I shan't do that! But he is good at what he does, even if he doesn't give a jot about human life.'

'Yeah, there was an actor who died, wasn't there? In his last film?'

'Yes. It was very tragic. Do you want

to go to the props department now?' asked Carmen.

Tony went with her to props but they could only repeat what she had told him. They would have used coloured water, or even just plain tap water.

'Surely you remember which?' Tony asked the head of the department. 'For continuity and all that?'

'Yes, it will be written down somewhere.'

'It was coloured water, for the record,' said Tony. 'That's what the police report said.'

'Right, then that's what we used,' said the props guy. Before Tony could ask any more, George Cassius sent a runner, demanding they go and dress the next set.

'Do you want to watch the filming?' asked Carmen.

'Yes, why not?'

Tony followed her to the sound stage and immediately regretted it. The set was a huge bed full of Egyptian furnishings. Patty and Matt were snuggled up in bed together and they looked as if they were naked.

Tony glanced around, wondering where Jude was, as he did not think the child should be around for this scene. He saw him through the sound stage door, sitting in a trailer with his tutor and poring over some books, in such a position that he could not see any of the scenes taking place.

Tony realised he should have given Patty more credit for making sure her son was safely out of the way. Someone shut the sound stage doors, closing Jude and his tutor out completely.

'I love you,' Patty, as Cleopatra, said to Marc Antony, her eyes glowing with passion. 'I've always loved you.'

There was a pause and then they kissed. It was the hottest thing Tony had ever seen and he would have given anything not to see it. Now he knew what they meant when they said actors working together had chemistry. There was definitely chemistry between Patty and Matt. He fought the compulsion to go and knock the big Australian out. Instead he held his breath, wondering with growing horror if they were about to film some explicit love-making. He wished he could be with Jude, reading text books, yet curiosity and perhaps some masochistic streak kept him glued to the spot.

'Cut,' said Cassius.

Tony breathed an audible sigh of relief. Patty got out of the bed and he saw that she was actually wearing a long white modesty sheet that covered her from just under her shoulders to her toes. Another woman came along, and for a moment he thought that Patty had a twin. Only, it was a twin who was less shy about being seen naked. The woman threw off her clothes with little ceremony. Matt got out of bed — he was wearing boxer shorts — and was replaced by a man who looked very much like him, except that the fair hair on Matt's body double was very obviously dyed.

Cassius ordered everyone but the

most necessary crew members to leave the set, for which Tony was extremely grateful. Even if the body double was not Patty, she looked too much like her for comfort. He knew then that even if the film did make it to the cinemas, he would never ever be able to watch it.

He watched as Patty and Matt went off to their respective trailers, walking close together and chatting quietly and looking far too comfortable. He was convinced that the kiss had ignited something in them, and it cut him to the core.

14

'We need to talk,' Patty said to Jude, as he munched pizza at the breakfast bar. Her mother and father were in another part of the house, and Patty was dressed for her dinner with Matt. She wore a plain black gown, which was offset with a scarlet shawl. Her cropped hair had been teased and was decorated with tiny gems that matched her delicate necklace.

'You look really nice, Mum.'

'Don't change the subject. You were very rude to Tony today. I didn't bring you up to be ill-mannered, Jude.'

'He made you cry.'

'I know that upset you, darling, but it's between me and Tony.' Patty rested her bare arms on the counter and reached out to her son. She spoke in gentler tones. 'Tony didn't ask to be your hero, sweetheart. It's a role you gave to him. So it isn't fair to say he's let you down.'

'He said he would help us.' Jude's big eyes looked up at his mother.

'And he did help us, didn't he? He took us somewhere safe so we wouldn't be bothered. He had a job to do, Jude, and he did that job. Just like when I go to the studio I have to act.'

'You really like him don't you?'

'I . . . ' Patty did not know how to answer that.

'Matt's much better for you. He's an actor, like you are. Like dad was.'

'Jude, don't make the same mistake with Matt as you did with Tony. Matt hasn't asked to be your hero either. I'm only going out to dinner with him to discuss what's been happening.'

'But you like him too, don't you?'

'Well, yes, I like him. He's a nice young man. I think he cared a lot about Olivia though, and I don't think he's ready to move on.'

'Are you, Mum?'

'Am I what?'

'Are you ready to move on after Dad?'

Patty thought hard about how to answer that one. She did not want to lie to her son and just tell him what he wanted to hear. 'Your father and I cared about each other a lot, Jude, but we fell out of love a long time ago. I'm very sorry that he's dead. I would not have wished it on him. But I'm not his widow. You understand that, don't you?'

'I know. That woman with the big . . .'

'Yes, alright, let's not go there, hey?' Patty stifled a giggle.

'I was going to say with the big lips!' Jude's face broke into a huge grin.

'Of course you were.'

'No, really, Mum. They could have been used as a lifeboat on the Titanic.'

'Jude!' Patty laughed despite herself. 'It isn't nice to be so rude about your father's ex-wife.'

'I just wonder what Dad saw in someone like her when you're so pretty, that's all.'

'Sometimes people are just not meant to be together. But your dad was one of my best friends, and more importantly he gave me you.' She ruffled Jude's hair. 'And I'll always love him for that. Now I want you to promise to be kinder to Tony when you next see him.'

'Alright,' said Jude, sighing. 'I suppose we're not really his problem, are we?'

'No, darling, we're not. And it's very mature of you to realise that.'

'Not whose problem?' Patty's father, Terence West, stood at the kitchen door. He was a big, handsome man with ginger hair and a resonant voice that had thrilled theatre-goers and commercial-watchers for years.

'Tony Marcus's,' said Jude.

'Oh, the detective blokey. It was rather nice of him to let you stay at his house, Jude.' Patty and her father exchanged glances. She had filled her parents in on everything that had happened.

'I know, Granddad.'

'So what are we doing tonight, lad?'

asked Terence. 'How about a game of tennis on that y-box thingy.'

'X-box, granddad. Not Y.'

'Whatever.'

'Can we watch *The Last Gladiator?*'

'No!' Terence and Patty said together.

'But all my friends at school have seen it.'

'That's up to their parents,' said Patty, who took very little stock by such utterances as 'everyone else has done it'. 'Whilst I'm your mother, you're not watching it. Maybe when you're older, hey?'

'So,' said Terence, clapped his hands together. 'The Y-box it is.' He winked at his daughter.

'X, Granddad, X!' Jude rolled his eyes. 'Honestly,' he said with a troubled sigh. 'Old people.'

'Oh dear.' Margaret West entered the kitchen much as she entered the stage: with a flourish. Now in her sixties, she was still as beautiful as when she starred in a renowned soap opera in the nineteen seventies. She had let her hair grow out to natural grey, and it hung on her shoulders glossy and clean, making her look like a good witch from legend. 'Is Granddad being silly again, darling?' She said it as 'dahling', with the vowels lengthened to infinity.

'A bit, Grandma,' said Jude. He smiled at Terence as if to show he did not mean to be unkind.

'Come on, lad,' said Terence. 'Finish your pizza and we'll play some tennis. Or,' he whispered conspiratorially, 'we can watch some DVDs.'

'Dad . . . ' Patty said in warning tones. 'I said he couldn't watch it.'

'I know you did, and I'd never go against you,' said Terence. But Patty was not convinced. Her parents had a rather relaxed attitude to nudity, often going off to naturist beaches to let it all hang out. It had mortified Patty when she was growing up and as a result, she had vowed never to do a nude scene in films and had shielded Jude from it. She supposed her parents' attitude was healthier, but she could not fight off the feeling that some things should be private.

Later that evening she sat opposite Matt in an Italian restaurant, telling him all about her parents.

'They sound wonderful,' he said.

'They are, though they're very naughty, both of them, when it comes to Jude. They can't deny him anything.'

'My parents weren't actors so don't really understand what I do. They're proud of me and all that but, they don't think of it as a proper job.'

Patty smiled. 'I was lucky not to have that problem. In fact, I rebelled for a while and went to sixth-form college, determined to be a secretary or something. Then I somehow got dragged into the drama productions at the college and overnight I realised why my parents loved it so much. What did your mum and dad want you to do?'

'My dad's a vet, so they thought I'd follow in his footsteps.'

'Where does he practise?'

'In Alice Springs. I used to help him

out during the lambing season.'

'That must be wonderful.'

'It's messy,' said Matt with a smile. 'But it was fun. Dad has his own small plane to get around. You need it in Australia. So I learned to fly when I was quite young.'

'Wow! So how did you get into acting?'

'Same as you. I went to college to study to be a vet, and got involved in the drama group. I gave up veterinary studies after the first year and went to drama school instead. Dad was disappointed, I think, but he's a cool guy. And I think Mum told him to let me do what I wanted in the hopes that one day I'd go back to the family business.'

'Do you want to?'

'Some days, working with George Cassius . . . I do think sheep are more attractive.' Matt laughed and Patty joined in. She was surprised to find that she was enjoying his company. He was stupidly handsome, but there was more to him than good looks and a brawny body. He was smart and funny too. A man with brains and a sense of humour went a long way with Patty.

'So,' she said, reminding herself why they were there. 'About what's been happening . . .'

'Yeah.' Matt's smile dropped. 'I can't work it out. I've tried. But there's nothing that links Jason, Andy and Olivia.'

'No,' Patty said. 'Jason and Andy have been in things together, but Andy was very much a bit-part actor at the time. And Jason has worked with Olivia before. But Andy and Olivia didn't know each other, as far as we know. And there's nothing that puts all three of them in the same place at the same time.'

'Do you know,' said Matt, frowning, 'I really think we're just dealing with a madman here.'

'That was my thought,' Patty agreed. 'And they're the hardest to catch, if there's no motive.'

'Cassius is plumb crazy.'

'Yes, he is. But is he a killer? I hate to say this, but whilst I can imagine him killing off less important crew members to get publicity, I can't imagine him killing off Jason.'

'That's got loads more publicity, Patty.'

'Yes, I appreciate that, but even so, Jason can — could — carry a film like few actors can. His name on the billboard ensures good box office receipts, and he was really good with the promotional side of things. I can't carry a film, even though I'm fairly successful at what I do. And with respect . . . '

'No, it's fine,' said Matt. 'I know I'm untried in films.'

'He needed Jason to make it really work. Even though Jason had done most of his scenes, they've had to put a lot more effort into adding him into scenes using computer graphics. Not to mention all the extra scenes we've had to film to account for his absence. It doesn't make sense that Cassius would shoot himself in the foot like that. He would surely have waited till Jason had filmed his final scenes, and it was all in the can.'

'But again, Cassius is a madman, Patty. He doesn't think like other people think.'

'That's true. I hate this.' Patty pulled at the paper napkin, tearing it to shreds. 'It's awful to suspect people. I look at everyone in the film crew and wonder if they did it.' She glanced up at Matt and saw him looking back at her intently. Something about the expression in his eyes unnerved her. Did he suspect her? That was probably why he asked her out — to test her. That was the worst thing about it all — not knowing whom she could trust and not knowing if people trusted her.

She thought of Tony and how he had looked at her from time to time, as if he were also wondering. Did she look like a killer? She was an actress, so technically she could be anything she wanted to be if it suited her purpose.

But acting and doing were two different things. It was something the public did not always realise. Patty remembered playing a bitchy bad girl once, against an actress who was universally accepted as a nation's sweetheart. For a while afterwards, she had received nasty letters from the other actress's fans. They were furious with her for words and actions that were only part of her performance in the film. It was ironic, because during filming the 'sweetheart' had been an absolute nightmare to everyone, including Patty. Maybe, she thought at the time, it was why her own performance had been so convincing — because she was projecting the actress's own behaviour back at her. The attempted murder scene had certainly been cathartic.

'Do you want another drink?' Matt asked, after a few moments of awkward silence.

'Yes, why not?' She put on her brightest smile, to prove to him that she was a nice woman who would never murder anyone. 'Tell me all about your father's plane.'

* * *

'I don't know if she'll do it, Dad.' Tony drove through London, talking to his father on the speakerphone.

'Tell her it's for a good cause,' said Harry. 'The local hospice does wonderful work.'

'I'm sure she'll appreciate that,' said Tony. 'But I just wonder what you're up to. Patty and Jude did not exactly leave Fazeby Hall under happy circumstances.'

'I'm not up to anything. Apart from maybe using your contacts in show business to drum up more interest in the fête. Will you ask her?'

'Yes, I'll ask her. I've got to go, Dad. I'm meeting George Cassius for a drink.'

'Namedropper! Maybe he'll open the fête.'

'Believe me, Dad, you don't want this guy around. He's an immense egotist, and I'm not sure he's nearly as clever as they say. You know that song Mum used to sing to me? About the Emperor's new clothes?'

'Yes.'

'Well it's like that with him. He's somehow fooled people into thinking he's an *enfant terrible*, and a genius. It seems to me that 'genius' is a word that's bandied about too easily nowadays. Someone makes one good film, or writes one good book or sings one good song, and suddenly they're a genius. Mostly they're a one-trick pony, and that's what Cassius seems to have been. In fact, I can't find anywhere where anyone other than himself says he's a genius. Everyone I've spoken to says, '*They* say he's a genius', which is not the same thing. But I can't find out who *they* are. He had a bit of success early on, but he's never been able to build upon it. I think he got lucky. He had Jason Carter as the lead in that first film, a really great scriptwriter and a group of solid supporting actors. Then it went to Cassius's head and he forgot that he wasn't alone in making that film good. He started thinking he was God. And that frightens me.'

'Do you think he's a killer, son?'

'That's what I want to find out. He's definitely unhinged.'

'Be careful. We've lost one son, and we've only just got you back from the wilderness.'

Tony smiled at the speakerphone. Los Angeles was hardly a wilderness. 'I can take care of myself, Dad.'

'I know you can, but please allow me to worry about you. Are you coming home for the weekend? Your mother would like to see you again before you head off back to America.'

'I'll see what I can do. Get in the fatted calf, eh?'

They said their goodbyes and Tony pulled into the underground car park of the luxury hotel where George Cassius was staying during filming.

'Come in,' said Cassius when Tony reached the suite. The man who met him was not the same man he saw at the studio. Something about him was different. 'What can I get you? Tea? Coffee? Something stronger? I've got a nice single malt if you're interested.'

Tony stared hard at Cassius. He was actually being charming, and even seemed a bit scared of Tony.

'I'd better stick to coffee, thanks. I'm driving,' said Tony, when he had digested this new information about Cassius.

'Coffee it is,' said Cassius. 'Sit down, Mr Marcus. Or may I call you Tony?'

'Tony is fine.'

'And I'm George.'

Tony sat down on a square leather sofa, wondering at the startling change in Cassius's behaviour. He looked around him. The suite was decorated in the art deco style, with walnut cabinets and lots of glass and chrome surfaces. Even his parents could not afford a suite this good in a London hotel. Most of their money went on keeping Fazeby Hall maintained. He felt a pang of regret for not helping them more. His mother deserved a stay in a luxury hotel. Not that Fazeby Hall was a dump. But it was a money pit.

'Nice suite,' he said, whilst Cassius poured the coffee.

'Yes, I like it. One has to be comfortable when working away from home.'

'Where is home for you, George?'

'I live along the M4 corridor, when I'm not at my place in Malibu.' There was a boastful element in Cassius's voice, which reassured Tony that the egotist was still in there somewhere.

Tony was perplexed. 'Yet you stay in a hotel whilst you're working south of London?'

'It's the wife. She says I'm unbearable when I'm working.'

Tony did not disabuse him of that notion. It tied in with what everyone said about Cassius. 'So you retreat here?'

'Yes. I miss the kids though. The school run and all that. I did a lot of it when I was out of work.'

'Must have been hard to be boycotted by the studios,' said Tony.

Cassius's eyes flashed momentarily. ''Boycotted' is a strong word. They just don't understand my vision.'

'What is your vision, George?'

'To make films that people need to watch rather than films they want to watch.'

'I don't get you. Can you explain what you mean?'

'They're fed on a diet of pap all the time. Bruce Willis shooting terrorists, *Batman*, *The Avengers Assemble*. All that comic book rubbish.'

'Don't people want to watch those films because they're enjoyable?' asked Tony.

'It's all fake,' said George, sitting on the arm of one of the sofas. 'It's not real film-making. It's just pandering to the masses. I sobbed when I saw the last Jason Carter film — that rubbish set on a train. It's all a load of sentimental tosh, aimed at the lowest common denominator, and he was better than that. We should make people think when they go the movies.'

'Personally speaking, George, I don't always want to think too much when I watch a film. I go to relax. I thought the last Jason Carter film was okay.' Tony did not admit that he had only recently caught up on all Jason Carter's films, as a way of getting a handle on the dead man. 'And Carter had charisma in his films. I enjoyed watching it.'

'That's where you're wrong, Tony. You weren't really enjoying that film. Not properly or on any deep and meaningful level.'

'Right . . . ' said Tony, who was pretty sure he had enjoyed the film. 'So all this sex and violence in the *Cleopatra* film . . . that's deep and meaningful.'

Cassius's eyes flashed again, but he did not rise to the bait. It was perplexing to say the least. True, George's ideas about film were extreme, but he spoke in balanced tones and not with the fire and brimstone he used on the film set. 'What did you want to see me about, Tony?'

'I wanted to ask if you had any idea

who might have killed Jason Carter, Andy Paxton and . . . ' To his shame he struggled to remember the make-up girl's last name. 'Olivia Cooper.'

'Someone who's trying to destroy me, that's who.'

'Yes, you said that. But do you have any specific names?'

'Everyone hates me. I don't care that they hate me — that's what happens when you're successful — but they do.' Despite his words, Tony suspected that Cassius cared very much. A man who tried so hard to annoy people had to care what they thought. It was the only way he could get a reaction out of them. For a man like George Cassius, who was like a child crying 'Look at me, Mummy', even a negative reaction was better than no reaction at all.

'But who hates you, George?'

'Everyone.'

'Aren't you being a bit paranoid?'

'I've told you. People don't understand my vision. 'Oh, George Cassius is a genius', they say, but none of them will work with me, because they can't hack it. They're afraid of delving deep and finding out how the world really is. They'd rather have their chick-flicks and their monster movies. Rubbish, all of it.'

It was then that Tony realised where the myth about George Cassius being a genius came from. He had started it himself, by mentioning some shadowy but unnamed people who thought he was talented. Admittedly, the studio must have bought into the myth, to give him free rein with the *Cleopatra* film, but how much of that was a result of George Cassius being his own best public relations expert?

'But not all movies are bad,' said Tony. 'There are some very thoughtful and intelligent movies out there. Like Ben Affleck's *Argo*. Or *The Hurt Locker*. People do go to see intelligent films.'

'If you call those intelligent,' Cassius scoffed. 'It's the Emperor's New Clothes, isn't it?'

Odd that he voiced exactly what Tony

had been thinking about him. Rather than sounding fiery and angry, Cassius sounded like a man defeated by his own shattered dreams. Tony wondered if the director, who was clearly delusional, would ever realise those dreams. He suspected that for Cassius the goalposts of what constituted a good movie would keep moving, and his own ideas of perfection would get bigger and less attainable. That way he could always blame someone else for his own failings. If the studio did not hire him, it would be their fault for not recognising his talent. If people did not watch his movies, it would be their fault for watching what Cassius called rubbish, and not his fault for failing to make the films they wanted to see.

'So you can't give me the specific name of anyone who would hate you enough to want to take this film away from you by killing three of the crew?'

'I've told you, Tony, everyone.'

Tony sighed, and wondered if Cassius had ever had counselling. He was the most paranoid man Tony had ever met. Or maybe it was part of his means of drawing attention to himself. The man thought the world revolved around him. 'That's not really much help, George. I'm sure you want to find who the killer is as much as anyone.'

'I suppose so.'

'You suppose?'

'I'm an artist, Tony. I can't be bothered with such trivialities.'

'I don't think Jude Carter thinks his father's death is trivial,' said Tony, his hackles rising. 'And I'm sure Andy Paxton's twin sons don't think so either. Nor Olivia Cooper's family.'

'You know what I mean. You're just twisting my words.'

Tony did not know how else he could take Cassius's words. The man was a cold fish and that was a fact. It made Tony wonder where all the heat came from whilst Cassius was filming. Could it be the man really was one big fake?

'Did you notice anything odd at the studio on the days they died? A crew member who was somewhere they shouldn't be? Or someone on set who should not have been there?'

'I wasn't really looking.'

'Tell me about the things that have happened in the past. You say the studio is hard on you, and that people wish you ill. Could it be linked to something you've done in the past? What about the actor who died during your *Ben Hur* remake?'

'His family were well paid.'

'I'm sure that was a great comfort to them,' said Tony, his voice tinged with irony.

'Of course it was. It all comes down to money in the end. I'd work for nothing myself, but not everyone is like that.'

Tony looked around the luxury suite and wondered at the veracity of Cassius's statement. 'So what happened?'

'He died.'

'Yes, I got that part. What happened to bring about his death?'

'The man was careless and didn't

follow safety procedures during the chariot scene.'

'Wasn't that the charge levelled at you afterwards?'

'I told you, they're all out to get me.'

Tony did not want to take a trip down Cassius's paranoia lane again, so he changed tack. 'You say the family were paid off?'

'They received the insurance and I made a donation to the family, out of the goodness of my heart. I'm not a monster, Tony. The man had children.'

'So he was married?'

'Divorced, I think. There was a girlfriend, Carla.'

'What did she do?'

'Huh?'

'What did she do? For a living?'

'I don't know.' Cassius frowned. 'Why would I know what the girlfriend of an actor did?'

Tony was about to ask more questions when the telephone rang. 'Excuse me,' said Cassius. He went to the phone and Tony noticed how he lowered his voice. 'Yes, Lombardi's. Yes, both of them. Make sure you get a good picture.' He put the phone down and turned back to Tony. 'Is that all, Tony?'

'Yes,' Tony nodded, realising he was not getting anywhere with George Cassius. 'That's all.'

Cassius saw him out and bid him a fairly civil goodnight. The man was a paradox.

Tony went to his car and did a search on his Satnav for a restaurant called Lombardi's. He had a hunch that Cassius was up to something and he wanted to be there to see if it was true.

15

Patty and Matt had been chatting quite happily when she looked up and saw Tony enter the restaurant.

'What . . . ' she said, frowning in his direction.

'Hello,' he said with a sheepish grin. She tried to tell herself that his smile meant nothing to her and that Matt's was much nicer. Still, she felt her tummy give a bit of a jolt. 'I thought I'd join your conference if you don't mind.' He pulled a chair up to the table without asking.

'We're kind of busy,' said Matt.

'Yes, trying to find out who the killer is, no doubt.' Tony was talking too loudly, and drawing the attention of everyone around him.

'Actually we were,' said Patty. She did not tell him that they had lost track of that discussion half an hour before and had instead talked about Matt's home life in Australia.

'That's what I thought. Two good friends, together, just trying to make sense of the awful tragedies around them.'

Patty looked at him, perplexed by the way he had accentuated the words 'good friends'. 'What is it to you?' she muttered under her breath.

'Absolutely nothing,' he said, staring at her blankly. The words cut through her. He lowered his own voice. 'But Cassius just tipped off the press that you were here and they're waiting outside.'

'He did what?' said Matt, looking around alarmed. 'How do you know?'

'I was with him when he did it. I didn't know it was definitely you, but I guessed it might be, so I came here as soon as I could. I know Patty likes to keep her private life private.'

'You do?' said Patty.

'I do.'

'Thank you.'

'Yeah, thank you,' said Matt, but he

did not sound as certain about it as Patty.

'I bet he was the one who sent the press to my house the other week,' she said.

'I'm guessing that's the case,' Tony agreed. 'He's a desperate man who needs all the publicity he can get.'

'The swine! So what do we do?' she asked. 'I don't suppose you've got the helicopter handy.' She smiled, awkwardly.

'No, not tonight.' Tony said. 'But if you leave with two of us, they won't know who you're seeing.'

'No,' said Patty, her eyes widening in alarm, 'but they might make even worse inferences!'

'What does it matter?' said Matt. 'If they see us together and think we're in a relationship, so what?'

'It's not that I wouldn't want to be seen with you,' said Patty. 'Please don't think that.'

'Don't forget that Patty has a son, Matt,' said Tony. 'She doesn't want him reading stuff about her in the gossip columns.'

'No,' Patty agreed. 'It was bad enough that Jason spent so much time filling their pages.'

'Of course, I'm sorry,' said Matt. 'I forgot about Jude.'

Patty glanced at him sharply. 'Did you?' Realising she was being silly, she smiled. Why should Matt think about Jude? One dinner date did not mean he had to devote himself to her child's welfare. 'I suppose we were caught up in other things.'

'Talking about the murders, I suppose,' said Tony in a steely voice.

'Of course, the murders,' Patty said. 'What did Cassius say?'

'That everyone agrees he's a genius and the whole world is against him because of it.'

'That sounds par for the course. I'm not sure he's a murderer though.'

'No, having spoken to him alone, I'm not sure he is either,' Tony agreed. 'He makes a lot of noise, but actually he's a bit of a coward. He was terrified of me tonight.'

'That might be because he thinks you suspect him,' said Matt.

'It could be,' said Tony. 'But I don't think it was that. I think he needs an audience to be a bully. One to one, he just can't hack it. He was almost civil to me.'

'I'd have loved to be a fly on the wall for that,' Patty said. 'Anyway, how are we going to get out of this restaurant?'

'What if Matt leaves first, then you and I leave together? It'll confuse them if nothing else.'

Patty pondered the idea for a moment. It might work. Tony was unknown and the media were never really interested if a celebrity was involved with a nobody. They liked pictures of celebrities together. 'We could try. If you don't mind, Matt?'

'I don't think I've got much choice,' said Matt sombrely. 'I'll get the bill.'

The bill dispensed with, Matt stood up to say good night. He nodded briefly at Tony, then reached across and kissed

Patty on the cheek. 'I had a really nice time,' he said. 'It was great to talk about home.'

'I enjoyed hearing about it.'

'We'll do it again sometime.'

'Yes, we must. Thank you, Matt.'

'Home?' said Tony, when Matt had left.

'His father is a vet in Australia. He has his own small airplane.'

'I thought you'd met to talk about the murders.'

'We did, but we didn't have a clue how to proceed. Being a sleuth doesn't really suit me. I prefer to see the good in people.'

'Even George Cassius?' Tony raised an eyebrow.

'George is just a little boy who didn't get enough attention from his mother.'

'You're a really forgiving person, Patty. First Jason, then George.'

'I didn't forgive Jason. I just learned to accept that he was what he was.'

'A man who cheated on you while you were pregnant.'

225

'I'm aware of his deficiencies, Tony, and you don't really need to remind me of what was one of the darkest times of my life. We'd better go.'

'No, it's too soon. I'll order more wine.' Tony called a waiter over and ordered another bottle. 'I'm sorry,' he said, when the waiter had gone. 'I imagine it must have been hard for you.'

'You always do that.'

'Do what?'

'Say horrible things then think an apology and a flash of that smile will get you out of trouble. It doesn't work like that. I don't think any man has ever hurt me as much as you sometimes do. Not even Jason.' The moment Patty said it, she wished she had not. It revealed too much about her feelings. She thought back to half an hour earlier when she was chatting amiably with Matt. What you saw with Matt Archer was what you got. Nothing was complicated. Tony Marcus, on the other hand . . . She cared too much about what he thought of her and she allowed his words to cut too deep.

'I ... Patty ... ' Tony became flustered. 'I was about to say sorry again, but I guess that would be a waste of time after what you said.'

'Yes, it would.'

'Tell me about Jason. Tell me why he inspired so much loyalty in you when he was incapable of being loyal.'

'When you love someone you forgive their faults, even when common sense tells you that you shouldn't.'

Patty sat back as the waiter arrived with the wine. She let him pour her a glass even though she did not feel like drinking anymore.

'Were you so much in love with him?' Tony asked when the waiter had gone away again. She wondered why the answer mattered so much to him. Was it that he was looking for another motive for her to kill Jason?

She rested her elbows on the table and put her chin in her hands. 'Before we started filming, I watched the Liz

Taylor and Richard Burton *Cleopatra* film. It set me thinking about the real story of Cleopatra's relationship with both Caesar and Marc Antony.'

'I have no idea what that has to do with Jason, but I'll bite. What was the real story?'

'Their stories inspired people, because of the romantic element. She was a great woman who loved two great men. And in the end she — and Marc Antony — died for that love. Or so the story goes. It was all very Romeo and Juliet. I suppose that's where the idea of Romeo and Juliet comes from, though I don't know. There have been other lovers who died for love.'

'You don't think Antony and Cleopatra did die for love?'

'Yes, probably, but that wasn't all. It wasn't just love that bound Cleopatra with Caesar and Antony. It was a wish for world domination. They wanted to be like Alexander the Great and rule over all the earth. When she and Antony died, it wasn't just out of love. It was because they had failed at world domination, and did not want to face the consequences.' She smiled sadly. 'And now you're wondering what on earth this has to do with Jason.'

'I am. But I don't mind waiting. I could listen to you talking forever, Patty.' His voice was deep with meaning. She struggled to ignore how his words made her feel — like a jittery schoolgirl. Yes, things were much less complicated with Matt. In that relationship, she was the one with the upper hand.

'When I met Jason,' she said, licking her lips, which had become very dry, 'he was already on his way to world domination. Perhaps not in the invading Gaul and taking slaves sense, thank goodness, but he was the King of Hollywood. And he made me believe I could be his queen. Can you understand how seductive that is to an eighteen-year-old girl just starting out in her acting career? Now I've said that, you'll no doubt think that I only latched onto him to be famous, but that wasn't it.' She shook her head, denying a statement that Tony had not even made. 'I was bowled over by him, and I believed that together — because we loved each other — we could have the world at our feet. Because the world loves lovers, as Cleopatra's legend shows.'

She took a sip of wine, suddenly very thirsty. But it did not quench her thirst and she realised that her longing was for something else entirely. 'We had more in common with Elizabeth Taylor and Richard Burton than you'd realise. It wasn't just in that wonderful voice of Jason's, which could reduce me to a quivering pile of jelly. During the filming of the original film, Richard Burton was so ill that Elizabeth Taylor had to nurse him. That's how they fell in love. It was much the same with me and Jason. But although people thought he was an alcoholic, it was his epilepsy. I found him having a fit one day. He was having them a lot at that time, and

I kept his secret for him. We fell in love and married soon after filming finished. Then I became pregnant and what we both wanted changed. Jason still wished for world domination, but I didn't, not anymore. Yes, I wanted to work and be a good actress, but I also wanted to be a good mother. And no matter what society tries to tell women nowadays, they can't have it all. Something has to give. I was determined it would not be my love for my baby. Jason, on the other hand, was terrified about being a father. It would age him, he said. He claimed to be joking, and he never told me to get rid of Jude. I can't accuse him of that cruelty, and he became a good father eventually. But within weeks of me announcing my pregnancy, he was slap bang in the middle of a mid-life crisis, buying a new sports car and running around with Miss Centrefold of the pneumatic lips. I thought I carried all the earth I wanted to own in my tummy, and that was enough for me, but Jason still wanted the whole kit and caboodle. Do you understand?'

'Yes, I think so, Patty.'

'So the great love story was not a great love story after all. It became a sad story of two people who found out they wanted very different things in life. And thankfully nowadays no one expects you to die for love. You can just get divorced.' She laughed, but there was very little humour in it. 'I did love Jason then, but it was a love based on a dream, not on the everyday reality of family life. I still cared about him as a good friend, right up until he died, but I had woken up from that shared dream a long time ago because I found another dream that needed my attention more than Jason ever did.'

'Jude?'

'Yes, Jude. It's sad, because I think Jason realised in the end that he could share that dream if he wanted, but it was too late for us. Too late for him.' Patty was surprised to realise that a tear had rolled down her cheek. She had not really cried since Jason died, but now she did. Not so much for her loss, but for what Jason and her son had lost. 'He was a good father,' she insisted. 'If a little bit absent. But his career was always more important than anything else in his life. I don't feel that way.'

'You're a wonderful mother.'

'Oh, I'm a dreadful mother. If Jude turns out alright — and he shows every sign of doing so — it will be despite me not because of me.'

'All mothers think that. My Mum is the same.'

'Diana is a sweetheart and a much better mother than you deserve.'

'Yes, I'll concede that — which reminds me. I have been ordered by the old man to ask you if you'd like to open a fête at Fazeby Hall next month. Don't worry if you're too busy. I told him you might be.'

'Would you like me to come?' She looked at him hopefully.

'I may be back in the States by then, so it doesn't really matter to me.'

There you go again, she thought,

stabbing me in the heart. She immediately regretted sharing so many of her intimate thoughts with him. She clearly meant nothing to him. 'Oh, well tell him I'll do it.'

'Why?' It was Tony's turn to look hurt. 'Because I won't be there?'

'I didn't say that. We'll have finished filming this awful film by then, and I think Jude would like to see Fazeby again. If I can bring him with me?'

'I'm sure Mum and Dad would love it.'

'Good. Now we'd better go, hadn't we? Let the paparazzi have its day wondering who on earth you are.'

'I could tell them I'm your bodyguard. That's if you're worried about being seen with me instead of that big hulking Australian.'

'Yes, it is a bit of a comedown from a vet's handsome son to a duke's handsome son,' said Patty, her lips curving at the corners. 'But I've never been snobbish about these things.'

'I'm glad you think I'm handsome.'

'Are you glad? Because I sort of get the impression you don't care what I think.'

'What am I supposed to say, Patty? You've just been on a date with another man who's younger and better looking than me. Or is it your wish, like Cleopatra, to make the entire male population fall in love with you?'

'No,' she said quietly. 'I'd just settle for having one man in my life who loved me.'

16

Filming had not quite finished on the day of the fête. Cassius had insisted everyone return the week after to re-do some scenes because whilst he was happy to use computer graphics to put Jason Carter into the film, he was not willing to do that for Andy Paxton. Instead he had hired another actor.

'At least he's not trying to show Paxton's death scene like he did with that poor actor,' Patty said to her parents, before they all left for the fête. 'I just hope he still pays Paxton's wife.' Not that Cindy Paxton was short of money. She had appeared in several newspaper and magazine spreads, wearing a push-up bra and talking about 'The Man I Loved'. Even though she did not really approve, Patty could not blame her. She did have twin sons to bring up and school fees to pay. Cindy

had said something odd in one interview about opening your own door, and
Patty supposed she was doing just that.

As Terence and Margaret were 'resting',
the duke and duchess had invited them
to the fête. Patty was glad for the moral
support, because rather than the press
wondering who Tony was, they very quickly
found out. She suspected George Cassius
had something to do with that too, having
failed in his attempt to drum up publicity by feeding her and Matt to the media
lions. The news that Patty was opening
the Fazeby Hall fête had really set tongues
wagging, and there was talk of an impend-
ing engagement. She did wonder if the
fact of her parents attending might lead
to even more gossip.

The gossip columnists would be disappointed, thought Patty, as her father
drove them north to Fazeby. She had
not seen Tony since the night he turned
up at Lombardi's, and as far as she
knew he was back in America, having
completed his case for the insurers.

So it was with some surprise that she

saw him waiting on the steps of Fazeby Hall with his parents. He was dressed in jeans and an open-necked white shirt, which showed off his honey-toned skin to perfection.

'Hello,' she said.

'Hello.'

'I thought you were in America.'

'I was for a while, but now I'm back.'

'I can see that.' Her heart beat rapidly in her chest. Was this going to be another one of those days when he hurt her? She had hoped to avoid that. Or had she? If she were honest, she had also thought about him being there and what she would say to him if he was. It always went better in her head.

'We can all see that he's here,' said the duke with a grin. 'Honestly, you wait for your son to turn up for ten years then you can't get rid of him.' He looked very happy about it. 'It's good to see you again. And you, Jude.'

'Hello, Duke. Hello, Duchess,' said Jude. Then, remembering his manners, 'Hello, Tony.'

'Alright mate,' Tony said, looking at Jude affectionately. 'I'm really glad you're here. Are you going to introduce us to your grandparents?'

Jude proudly made the introductions, including a brief biography of both Terence and Margaret's recent theatre successes, which made everyone laugh.

'He sounds like Michael Parkinson without the Yorkshire accent,' said Terence, laughing. 'I'm very glad to meet you, Your Graces, and Lord Anthony.' The next few minutes were filled with 'so glad to meet you's and 'I've loved all your plays' and 'what a beautiful house' and other such pleasantries. Then they were taken to the drawing room for tea and scones, and Harry shared the day's itinerary.

'There's going to be a bit of a talent contest this afternoon, so I wondered if you'd mind doing the honours as the panel of judges. Nothing too unkind, of course. We don't want to ruin anyone's dreams.'

'That sounds like fun,' said Margaret.

'And I'm sure we'll both be very nice.' She looked sternly at her husband. 'Won't we, Terence? He does get rather carried away when the X-Factor is on, I'm afraid.'

'When we were starting out, you had to have an apprenticeship,' said Terence. 'And you expected to do it. Now they think they can be stars with five minutes of experience.'

'See what I mean?' said Margaret, rolling her eyes heavenward.

'I absolutely agree with Terence,' said the duke. 'Then they can't handle the pressure.'

'Oh good gracious, now you've started Harry off,' said Diana, laughing. 'Let's leave the men alone together to talk about how standards have fallen whilst I show you ladies around the grounds. We're having the fête on the big lawn, next to the Italian garden. Are you coming with us, Jude, dear? Or staying with the men?'

'I don't know . . . ' He looked a little unsure of himself.

'Tell you what, Jude, why don't I take you down to the village we talked about last time,' Tony suggested. 'If it's not too boring for you.'

'I'm very sorry if I was rude,' Jude said mechanically. 'I was having a bad day with my studies.'

'Algebra, eh?'

'Yeah, I'm rubbish at it.'

'Me too,' said Tony. 'So do you want to come?'

Jude looked to his mother and Patty immediately realised that all he wanted to do was please her. It made her heart swell. 'Yeah, alright then,' he nodded. 'Can Mum come too?'

'Yes, course she can. Unless she's needed . . . ' Tony looked to his mother for guidance.

'Oh, we'll be fine, Margaret and I,' said Diana. 'The fête doesn't start for another hour and a half. Just make sure you're back for the opening ceremony.'

'Oh I've written something,' said Patty, taking a folded sheet of paper from her handbag. 'Do you want to check it's suitable?'

Diana smiled. 'I'm sure it will be.' She took the paper anyway, and quickly perused it. 'Perfect,' she said. 'We are grateful to you for doing this, Patty. We know you've had much to contend with lately.'

'It'll be nice to spend the day thinking about something else,' said Patty.

She followed Tony and Jude from the room. The village was about half a mile from the Hall, and she began to wish she had worn more suitable shoes. 'I didn't realise I'd be trekking,' she said with a grimace.

'It's a fairly straight road,' said Tony. 'And it's dry enough.'

'Yes, the weather has kept nice, hasn't it?'

They talked about the weather for a while, and then all three fell into an awkward silence as they walked. Patty did not know what to say to Tony, and neither did Jude. It seemed that Tony did not know what to say to either of

242

them. It was a strange sort of triangle.

'I'm glad . . . ' Tony started to say.

'What were . . . ?' Patty said at the same time.

'Sorry, you go first.'

'No, you go first.'

'I'm glad you came today,' he said.

'Yes, it's a lovely day for a fête.'

'I'm glad you're here too, Jude. I know things didn't go to well last time you were at Fazeby.'

'It's alright,' said Jude. 'Mum said that you didn't ask to be my hero and she's right. You didn't. I was acting like a stupid kid.'

'Nah, you've never been stupid, mate. And I let you down. I know that.'

'Me and Mum are not your problem.'

'Maybe not, but friends look out for each other, don't they?'

'Anyway, it doesn't matter now,' said Jude. 'You had a job to do and you had to do it properly. I don't care about the insurance money and neither does Mum.'

'I'm not doing that job anymore,' said Tony.

'No?' Patty turned to look at him. 'I thought that's why you were in America.'

'I was, but not for Cassell and Keep. I gave my notice.'

'So what were you doing in America?' It was the question she had meant to ask in the beginning.

'Giving in my notice for a start. But I was also trying to talk to that actor's family and friends. You know, the guy who died in the *Ben Hur* remake?'

'Why?'

'I just had a hunch, but I wasted my time.'

'You don't think it's connected?' asked Jude, eagerly becoming the sleuth again.

'I can't find out for certain. It seems Cassius paid the family very well, and that included a gagging order. As I had no official capacity, they all refused to talk to me.'

'That's awkward,' said Jude thoughtfully. 'But thanks for trying, Tony.' He was looking at Tony with something like admiration again. Patty had wanted Jude to be friends with Tony, but she was also afraid of him getting hurt. She hoped that he would accept that Tony had done enough and not expect him to do any more.

'Here's the village,' said Tony.

'Mum, look! Isn't it brilliant?' said Jude, running forward towards two wrought iron gates.

The village was built behind a gated and very ancient wall. The gate was open, but there was a sign saying that it was locked at eight o'clock every evening and after that only those with a key could pass through.

As they had been told, all the cottages were like small castles, but each was built differently. Some had turrets, others had towers. All had gabled windows and were built from a mixture of red brick and Derbyshire stone. There was a quaint post office, and next door to that a tea room. 'My great-grandfather built the cottages for the estate workers,' Tony said as they walked around. 'He wanted every man to have his own little castle, and it was seen as a model village in its time, especially when most agricultural workers lived in a couple of rooms with enormous families all having to share sleeping space.'

'Do all the estate workers live here now?' asked Jude.

'Not all of them. We rent some cottages out to local professionals.'

'I bet they're worth a fortune,' said Patty. 'I know of a few people in London who would kill for country cottages like this.'

'Yes, which is why we have a strict residency rule,' said Tony. 'Dad doesn't want weekenders who won't bring anything to the local economy. Anyone living here has to work either locally or in the surrounding areas, like Chesterfield or Sheffield.'

'You said 'we',' said Patty. 'Does that mean you're involved now? Is this what you're doing now you've given up your job?'

'Yeah, yeah, it is,' Tony said, looking suddenly bashful. 'I don't have anything else doing at the moment, so I've come home to help my dad.'

'Tony, that's wonderful. No wonder he looks so happy.'

'I haven't said I'm staying.'

'I think you will,' she said gently. 'You look happier too.'

'I look happy today,' he replied meaningfully.

'Can we live in one of these, Mum?' asked Jude. 'I'd love my own battlements.'

'We wouldn't be allowed, darling. We don't live locally.'

'But we could.'

'Actually,' said Tony, 'the estate manager's house is now empty. He's just retired and moved to the coast with his wife. It's that one up there.' He pointed to one of the bigger houses. It was double fronted, with a balcony above the front door, like a mini version of the balcony on Buckingham Palace. It had its own clock tower above the balcony.

'It's charming,' said Patty.

'So when are we going to move in?' asked Jude.

She laughed to hide her discomfort.

'Not this week, darling. You have a term to finish at school and I have to find another acting job.' That was not strictly true. She had been offered lots of work in the wake of the murders during the filming of *Cleopatra*, but she had turned a lot down, feeling she could not cope with all the intrusion into her life that would surely result.

'A new film?' asked Tony.

'No . . . not really. I thought I'd do some theatre. People forget about you when you're in the theatre. Filmgoers do at least. If they don't see you at the movies every week or on television, they assume you've given up.'

'And do you like the idea of being forgotten?' asked Tony.

'Oh yes. Definitely.'

'So moving here would be ideal,' said Jude.

'Yes, it would,' Tony agreed. 'Jude could go fishing in the lake any time he wanted.'

'That'd be great.'

'We'd better get back,' said Patty,

looking at her watch. 'I have duties to perform.'

'Can we, Mum?' Jude whispered as they walked back.

'Shh,' she said. Her mind was in turmoil. Her son was vulnerable and she did not appreciate Tony upsetting him by tempting him with a rural idyll that they could not possibly take on. She did not think she could cope with living so close to Tony all the time. One day he would marry and carry on the family name. And she would have to witness it all if they moved to the village.

Yet she could not deny that it was a seductive idea, moving to that lovely house behind a gate that was locked every night to keep out all comers. But would that be the case if she moved there? She doubted it. Then the duke and duchess would be troubled by paparazzi trampling all over their beautiful estate. She realised she would have to explain all that to Jude when she had the chance.

Half an hour later she had completed her opening speech, thanking her hosts for their hospitality and welcoming the visitors to the fête.

The organisation was a work of art. Stalls had suddenly appeared with tombolas and shooting games, and there were arts and crafts tables. Her mother spent a fortune, and Patty bought far more than she intended. Jude had been charged with taking everything back to the car, piece by piece, which he did with gusto. The talent contest was fun, and though no one was very good, the audience gave everyone a standing ovation just for having the courage to get up there. Terence, who was not really an unkind man despite his earlier moans about falling standards, told everyone they were superstars in the making.

Once or twice, as Patty walked around, she saw Jude following Tony. At one point, Tony showed him how to use the rifle on the shooting game. It brought a lump to her throat, thinking that it was something Jude had never done with his own father, and never would be able to do. Jason was the type of father who threw money around rather than spending time with their son showing him how to do things. So their trips out consisted of visits to the toy store, to fill Jude's room up with a dozen more things that he might never play with, and then a trip to a burger bar or the movies. She could not remember if she had ever seen them as deeply in conversation as Jude and Tony were.

She shook off the feeling, knowing that like the idyllic cottage in the village, it was too seductive an image.

'A penny for them?' said Tony. She blinked quickly, not realising he had come over to her.

'I was just thinking that I haven't had such a nice day in a long time,' she said. It was not a lie. 'No one bothers me here. It's like they don't care who I am and treat me as if I'm normal. What am I saying? I am normal!'

'I'd say you were pretty extraordinary.'

'I'm not, Tony,' she said, earnestly. 'I'm not at all.'

'You're not going to say something about being just a girl looking at a guy hoping . . .'

She laughed. 'No!' And yet in that moment she understood exactly what Julia Roberts had meant when she said it to Hugh Grant in *Notting Hill*. Because it was hard to ask someone to just love you for yourself, when you could not separate the part of you that was famous.

'Have you seen Matt lately?' asked Tony.

His question seemed to make the sun shine less bright. 'No. I mean, I've seen him at the studio, but not socially. If that's what you meant.'

'Yes, that's what I meant. Patty?'

'What?'

'Can we go somewhere to talk?'

'Oh erm . . . where's Jude?'

'He's fine. My dad has taken him and your dad to see the orangery. I think our mums are off somewhere having their fortunes told.'

'That's okay then.'

He led her to a private garden behind the house. One that was closed off to the public, and surrounded by a high stone wall. 'Your great grandfather liked his walls, didn't he?' she asked, just for something to say.

'Yes, I suppose he did.'

They sat down on a wooden bench, and for a moment things were awkward between them again. 'I know you're going to hate me for saying sorry again,' said Tony, eventually. 'But I am sorry for mentioning Matt. I wanted you to forget about him today, and then I was the idiot who went and brought his name up. I know he's considered fairly gorgeous and hunky, but he's not right for you, Patty.'

'Oh? Why? Because he's younger?'

'Oh that's not an issue and you know it. You're only a couple of years older than he is, and you actually look younger. He'd be the luckiest man in the world to have you. That's why I have to know. Do you love him?'

'I . . . no . . . no, I don't think so.'

'You don't think so. You mean you can't say for definite.'

'Why does it matter?'

'Because if you love him, I'll back off. But I won't be happy about it. Because I don't think he's right for Jude either. And you need someone who cares about your son too. Oh I'm not saying he'd be unkind. He seems a good enough bloke. But I don't think he's ready to be a father. He didn't even consider the effect of you being in the press on Jude.'

'It wasn't his job to consider it. It was mine.'

'It's the job of anyone who wants to be involved with you, Patty. If they want to be part of your life they have to be part of your son's too.' He spoke emphatically and with passion.

'Do they?'

'Yes, they do. You're a package. Any sensible man should realise that.'

'But I don't generally expect men to commit themselves to a lifetime of fatherhood after one date.'

'So it was a date then? And not just to talk about the murders.'

'I don't know what it was, Tony. I never got a chance to find out. We were rudely interrupted, if you remember.'

He grinned sheepishly. 'Yeah, that was a bit embarrassing of me, wasn't it?'

'It was a bit. Why did you do it?'

'I told you why. Cassius had tipped off the press and I didn't want you caught up in it.'

'I'm not your problem, Tony.'

He half turned in the seat to face her. 'Patty, you've been my problem since the first day I saw you on set.'

'Have I?' she asked, feeling a little breathless. She considered herself to be an independent woman, who did not really need a man in her life. Yet here he was, acting all alpha and possessive. It was rather a new experience for her to feel like a helpless woman with a big strong man beside her. Yet had she not been that way since they met, letting him bring her to his parents to save her from the press? She knew she should fight it. Like Jude, she was in danger of making Tony into a hero and he had already proved that he was not comfortable in that role.

'Yes, you have. From that moment I wanted to protect you from anything that might harm you. And then I wanted to protect Jude too, because if you loved him, I loved him. I didn't even care if you'd killed Jason or not. I told myself that you must have had good reason. And even if you didn't have a good reason, even if it was for the money, I didn't care. I've been a selfish so-and-so for most of my life, but for the first time I had other people in my life who were more important than me. Now I want to be the sort of man you deserve. That's why I came back here; to take up the role Dad always wanted me to play.'

'If you think it matters to me that you

have a title, Tony, it doesn't.'

'But it matters to me now. I made a huge mistake ten years ago, Patty. I didn't fight for the woman I loved. I suppose that's because I didn't love her that much. I don't know. Now I'm determined I won't make that mistake again. That's why I crashed your date with Matt. If you tell me to get lost, I promise not to bother you again. But because of you, I know I can be a better man than I have been.' He stroked her cheek. 'You're so lovely.' His mouth was inches from hers, his warm breath gently blowing on her cheek.

It had been so long since she had been kissed. Really kissed, that was, and not screen kissed. She wanted to savour the anticipation of that moment, but she also longed to feel his mouth on hers. He was tentative at first, his lips brushing hers gently, exploring and seeking permission. When she sighed happily, his mouth took full possession of hers, as he crushed her to him. They stayed like that for what seemed both an eternity and yet was still far too short a time. He pulled away.

'So that's the difference,' he whispered.

'What?'

'I was so jealous when I saw you kiss Matt on the set. It looked real. But now I know it wasn't. I don't know, maybe because I'm on the other end of this kiss.'

'It's not the same,' she said, throatily. 'I promise you it's not.'

'Darling . . . ' he murmured against her cheek. They would have kissed again, but his mobile phone started to buzz in his top pocket. 'Damn,' he said, taking it out. He flipped it open and put it to his ear.

'Sam? Hi . . . ' He stood up and walked a few feet away. 'You have? When?' He listened for a while, and Patty wondered what was being said on the other end. 'Yes, she's here. I'll tell her. Thanks.'

'What is it?' she asked.

'Good news,' said Tony. 'I think it's good news, anyway.'

'What? Tell me!'

'They've arrested two men for the murders.' He looked perplexed, as if something did not make sense.

'What?' Patty felt suddenly faint. Relief washed over her, and it was only in that moment that she realised just how tense she had been over the previous months.

'Two men. Some old crook and one of the activists. They say they were in it together.'

Patty felt the world spin around her. 'Are you alright, darling?' asked Tony. 'You look ill.'

17

Vince Astwell and Peter Harris sat in separate interview rooms. Harris was a good-looking black guy in his late twenties, and Vince was a scrawny but tough man in his fifties. They had been brought in earlier that morning and questioned continuously for most of the day. Soon the police would have to press charges or let them go.

'We found CCTV footage of Peter Harris breaking the ranks of the protesters and climbing over a fence into the studio on the day Andy Paxton died,' Sam Brady explained to Patty and Tony, who had travelled down to find out what had happened. Jude and his grandparents had been invited to stay overnight at Fazeby Hall. They were in Sam's office. 'He says he was only leaving leaflets.'

'I remember getting one in my

trailer,' said Patty. Everything still felt dream-like and she was finding it difficult to wake up.

Sam nodded. 'We think that if he could get over then, he could have got over before. Harris and Vince Astwell did time together in prison. And guess who was in the same prison?'

'Andy Paxton?' Tony guessed.

'Yep. Peter Harris knew Paxton from the drama group. Vince was someone Andy knew from the outside. Vince was seen threatening Andy the day he died.'

'So why kill Jason and Olivia?' asked Patty. 'It doesn't make sense if their problem was with Andy Paxton.'

'It was a smokescreen perhaps, to hide their true intent. Or maybe they wanted to frighten Andy Paxton before finally killing him.'

'What do they say?' asked Tony, still looking puzzled. Patty knew that he felt as she did — that the truth had not yet been discovered.

'They deny it of course. Peter Harris admitted he knew Andy Paxton quite well, but insists he barely knew Astwell. He says his days of crime are behind him. He's involved with the activists because he says that, as a black man, he feels strongly about white people playing ethnic roles. But he also says that the theatre saved him. According to his rap sheet, that appears to be true. He was only in trouble that once, when he was nineteen, and only did six months in prison. But it's possible he just hasn't been caught.'

'Can we see the interview?' asked Tony.

'Not really,' said Sam. 'You know it's not allowed.' He spoke so emphatically that Patty had no doubt that Sam had bent the rules for Tony before. She wondered if it was during her interview, but decided it did not really matter any-more. They had two men and it looked as if those men would be charged.

'You don't seem happy, Tony,' said Patty. 'Don't you think they did it?'

'I just found out some things in America. I was about to tell you when the phone went.'

Patty did not remind him that they were smooching when the phone rang. 'What things?'

'It doesn't matter now.'

'It might,' said Sam. 'If you know anything, Tony, you need to tell me.'

'Matt Archer knew the actor who died on the *Ben Hur* film. The same guy had done a few episodes of *The Last Gladiator*.'

'So?' said Patty.

'I just wondered why he hadn't bothered to mention their friendship, that's all.'

'Because he probably thought it wasn't relevant, or he thought that people would know if they'd watched the series,' she suggested. 'You don't think Matt killed them all, do you?'

'I'm just saying that there are things he's kept quiet about.'

'You want him to be guilty,' said Patty, her eyes widening in surprise, 'because you're jealous of him.'

'That is not the reason.' Tony looked

angry. 'It's clear that you don't want him to be guilty.'

'I'd rather he wasn't, because he's a nice, decent young man,' she said. 'Tony, they've got the killers. Can't you be happy with that?' But why should he be, she thought, when she also knew without doubt that they had the wrong men?

'Are you satisfied that the men who wanted revenge on Andy Paxton would want to kill two innocent people?' Tony posed the question to Patty and Sam.

'It makes a bit more sense than Matt Archer killing them because the actor was his friend,' said Sam. 'Where is the motive in that?'

'I don't know. I haven't worked that out yet. But I know that actor's death had something to do with it. It was something Cassius said, only I can't remember what it was now.'

'We've got leave to question Harris and Astwell for a few more hours,' said Sam. 'I'm pretty sure this case is closed now, Tony. If you find out anything else, of course, I'd like to know.'

Tony and Patty left Sam's office. Their earlier intimacy had been forgotten and there was a strained atmosphere as they went to his car.

'I just don't think Matt would kill anyone,' said Patty, when they were driving away. 'It must be those two men. Who else would do that?'

'I can see you're determined to defend him.'

'Honestly, Tony, I thought you and I had dealt with all that stuff about Matt.'

'I just don't see why you have to stick up for him. I know that actor's death had something to do with all this.'

'And because Matt knew him, he's the obvious suspect?'

'He's the closest thing I've got to a suspect.'

'That's just wishful thinking.' She turned her head to look at him. 'Isn't it?'

Tony sighed. 'Maybe. I'm not satisfied with the way things have gone, I can tell you that.'

'Well I am, because now they have those two men in custody, I feel safe for the first time in months.' It was not strictly true, but she felt that if she said it, it might make her feel safer. She reached out and put her hand on his knee. 'So can we stop arguing about Matt? Because I've just realised that Jude has four babysitters, and what's more is over two hundred miles away, and his nanny is away on holiday. I feel like celebrating.'

'In what way?'

'My goodness, you're slow on the uptake, Lord Antony.' She squeezed his knee. 'It means my house is completely empty.'

'Oh.' He turned to smile at her.

'Of course, if you really hated our kiss . . . '

'I assure you I did not. But I do suspect you're trying to change the subject.'

'Okay, let's talk about the case instead.'

'I didn't say you couldn't change the subject. I just said you were obviously trying to.' He took her hand and raised it to his lips. 'Let's go and explore that big empty house of yours, shall we?'

They managed to explore every room in one way or another. It was a long time since Patty had entirely given herself up to such pleasure and she savoured every moment in Tony's arms. By the morning she had almost convinced herself that the danger was over.

The following afternoon, Jude and his grandparents, who had been invited to spend the night at Fazeby, returned to find Patty and Tony sprawled over each other on the sofa in the kitchen.

'You look happier, darling,' said Margaret, blowing her daughter a kiss.

'It's all over, Mum,' she said. Patty sat up and held her arms out to Jude, who gave her a kiss, then sat between her and Tony. But he looked as happy as she felt. She put her arm around his shoulders. 'And you don't have to worry about me anymore, sweetheart.'

'Yes, we saw they'd charged the two men with murder,' said her father.

'Tony isn't happy about it,' said Patty. 'He'd like to lock poor Matt Archer up.'

'A man can't cope with too much competition,' said Tony. 'Especially in the form of a stupidly handsome Australian.'

'He's not that good-looking,' said Jude.

'Oh he is,' said Patty mischievously. Her good mood made her playful, and she hoped that she had given Tony enough proof of her affection the night before.

'Yes, I'd say so too,' said Margaret.

'They're ganging up on us, Jude,' said Tony.

'Yes, but we're three against two with Granddad.'

'Keep me out of it,' said Terence. 'I've never won an argument with your grandmother in thirty-five years of marriage.'

The rest of the day passed by very happily. They all ate a big dinner together, and Tony agreed to stay another night. It was like being a proper family, thought Patty as they played board games and laughed and joked with each other.

She had to believe that the darkness which blighted their lives since Jason's death had gone. Yet at one point she shivered. It was all too easy, the men being arrested. Perhaps, she thought, she was too used to films where there was always a final explosive scene involving all the main characters. The arrest of Peter Harris and Vince Astwell had taken place offstage, and as such seemed anticlimactic. But perhaps that was just real life.

In the morning she would return to work and all would be back to normal. Once again she shivered, and became convinced that she was not yet safe. That night she clung to Tony again, determined to grasp at every bit of joy she could before it was too late.

18

It seemed to Patty that once the two
men were in custody, the wheels of
justice ground to a halt. The police
questioned everyone again, to find out
if anyone had noticed if Astwell and
Harris had been around the studio. All
had seen Peter Harris amongst the
protesters, but no one remembered
seeing him on the set.

She was particularly moved by Peter
Harris's grandmother, who had brought
the boy up alone. Interviewed for television news, Mrs Astwell said, 'It's true
that Peter got into trouble in his youth,
but the theatre and acting saved him.
He just feels strongly that white men
and women should not be playing ethnic
characters. But he's not a killer. Not my
Peter.' The woman's conviction was heart-
breaking to see.

'It's so sad,' Patty said to Tony one

evening as they ate dinner at her house. Jude had eaten his food and gone upstairs to watch television in his bedroom. Margaret and Terence were out seeing the opening night of a friend's show. 'That poor woman. She obviously did her best for her grandson. She must have thought she'd succeeded, after his first bit of trouble with the police.'

'You're not sorry that Jason's killers have been arrested, are you, darling?' he asked.

'No, of course not. I wouldn't like to see an innocent man going to jail, that's all. The protesters weren't violent. They were noisy, yes. But they behaved well enough and only ever tried to put their point across in a civil way, as far as I could see. I can't believe anyone feels strongly enough about it to kill three people.'

'What are you afraid of?' he asked, reaching across to take her hand.

'I suppose I can't believe it's over, and in such a quiet way. That's actresses for you,' she said, trying to raise a smile.

'We expect big explosions and all that. Or even a car chase.'

'Maybe the big court scene will be closure for you, my love,' he said, raising her hand to his lips, and kissing her palm in a way that made her feel giddy with excitement.

'I'd forgotten about that. Yes. That will be it. The final verdict.' She felt more relaxed. Tony was right. As soon as the two men had been properly convicted, she would feel safe again.

'Is that the name of a film?'

'If it isn't, it should be.'

'Well this one has certainly had it all,' said Tony. 'The murders, the misunderstandings between lovers, the love rival . . . '

'A bit melodramatic though, don't you think?'

'Isn't that how you want it to be?'

'I'm not sure I do. Even though this is all a bit of an anti-climax, I actually prefer the quiet life. I've told you. I don't want world domination. It's far too exhausting.'

'When this is really over — ' Tony started to say. The ringing of the house phone disturbed him.

'Saved by the bell,' Patty quipped, wondering what he had been going to say, and whether it was what she had longed to hear. Life was still too uncertain to make any solid plans. When the two men were locked up securely, maybe then.

She picked up the phone. 'Patty?'

'Yes?'

'It's George. George Cassius. Will you come down to the studio? I'd like to do some more filming.'

Patty frowned. 'George, it's nine o'clock.'

'I know, and I'm sorry to bother you.' The hairs on the back of her neck prickled. 'But it's important we do this one last scene. Then I promise you'll be free of me forever.'

'That sounds a bit drastic. Can't it wait?'

'No,' he said, 'it can't bloody wait!'

'Ah, there you are, George,' she said, feeling strangely relieved. 'Very well. If I have a promise you won't bother me again, I'm on my way.'

'Good. Thanks.'

She put the phone down and turned to Tony. 'George wants to film a final scene. I wonder . . . I can't take Jude with me at this time of night. Do you mind taking care of him, darling?'

'No, it's no trouble. Are you alright, love? You look worried.'

'Oh I'm fine. It's just that George was being nice and he's never nice.'

'He was to me when I was with him,' said Tony. 'Well, as nice as he can be. I think he's like that on a one-to-one level. He's only loud when he has an audience. Leave Jude with me. We'll have a great time together.'

'You mustn't let him watch *The Last Gladiator*.'

'Oh don't worry, there's not much chance of that,' Tony said wryly.

Patty went back to Tony, who was still sitting at the table, and put her hands on his shoulders. She kissed the tip of his nose. 'You never really had to worry, you know. About Matt, I mean.'

'Any man with common sense would worry about that big handsome devil. Do you think they make them like that in a factory in Sidney? Churning out blond Adonises with too much in the abs department?'

'Now you're being unkind!'

'I know. It's my basic insecurity.' He put his arms around her waist and pulled her in tight. 'When you get back, you'll just have to convince me about how wonderful you think I am.'

'Did I say that?' she teased. 'I don't remember saying it.'

'You said lots of things in the throes of passion.'

'So did you, as I remember. In fact I couldn't shut you up!' She touched his lips lightly with hers, and immediately wished she had told George Cassius to get lost.

'We'll have to practice those scenes again later. Make sure we get all those words absolutely right.'

'I can hardly wait.'

'In that case,' he said, patting her lightly on the bottom, 'get the hence to the studio, woman, and don't keep me waiting too long.'

* * *

It was with some regret that Tony waved Patty off. But he had made a promise to himself that he would not stand in the way of her career. If she wanted to work, then he would support her in every way possible.

He wandered upstairs to find Jude. He was not watching television. Instead he was sitting at his computer, browsing the internet.

'What's up, mate?' asked Tony. 'Mum's had to go to work, so it's just me and you.'

'It's a bit late,' said Jude, glancing casually over his shoulder.

'Yeah, I know, but George Cassius promised never to darken her doorstep again and I think that was too good an offer for her to pass up. So what are you doing? I wondered if you fancied watching some telly. Or we could play a computer game together? What is it that you bright young things like to do of an evening?'

'You sound like my granddad.' Jude laughed.

'Thanks!'

'Yeah, you're old, but not that old.'

'Well just hang on a minute whilst I go and get my arthritis pills and Complan! So what do you say, mate? Is it telly? A computer game? Or, 'Get lost Tony, I've got my own thing going on with a pretty girl in France'?'

'I wish,' said Jude. 'Nah, I'm still doing some detecting work. Since you and Mum seem to have given up.'

'We haven't given up, mate,' said Tony. He sat on the edge of the bed, resting his elbows on his knees. 'The two men have been arrested.'

'It's not them,' said Jude. 'I know it isn't. Mum knows it isn't either. That's why she's still not happy.'

'Jude,' said Tony cautiously. 'Sometimes

it doesn't do to delve too deeply. You might not like what you find out.'

'You don't still think Mum did it, do you?' Jude spun around on his chair. 'I thought you loved her.'

'I do love her. But . . . '

'But you still think she could kill someone?'

'No . . . actually, I don't, Jude.' For the first time, Tony realised that was true. He had wondered for a long time about Patty, even after he had begun to love her. But knowing her, sharing her life and her bed, had proved to him that she was not capable of such violence. Of course, he might be blinded by love, but he doubted it. There was nothing small or petty about Patty, and in Tony's experience, those who killed often did so for small and petty reasons. Oh they dressed it up as passion or compulsion, but it generally came down to getting more money or removing an obstacle to something else they wanted. Patty had no reason to do that with Jason. She earned her own money and her ex-husband had been more than generous with Jude, and also a good friend to her once the rancour of their divorce was over. 'I don't think your mum is a killer,' he said, more certainly.

'So what are you afraid I'll find out?'

'Oh I don't know. I mean . . . you liked Matt, didn't you?'

'He was alright. But if he turned out to be the man who killed my father I should stop liking him straight away.' It was said with a child's innocence and sincerity. 'So do you think he did it? Or is it just wishful thinking because he likes Mum?'

'Did I ever tell you that you're far too clever for your age?' Tony laughed. 'It's really very annoying. No one likes a kid who's a smart alec.'

'You do like me though, don't you, Tony?' Jude looked a little bit hurt.

'What? Of course I do, mate! I was kidding.' Tony wanted to kick himself. For all Jude's brains, he was still just a child who took things at face value. 'For the record, I love you and your mum.'

'So you're not just being nice to me to suck up to her then.'

'No. You're the nicest kid I've ever met and one day I hope ... ' Tony stopped. He could not say anything to Jude until he had spoken to Patty properly.

'Yeah, so do I,' said Jude with an elated smile. 'That would be brilliant! So will you help me to do some detecting then?'

'Why not? If we can get Matt Archer locked up between us, it'll be worth it.'

Jude sighed and rolled his eyes. 'You must have been a rubbish detective. You're supposed to go into things with an open mind.'

'Okay, Watson. What have we got so far?'

'I've been thinking about the bloke who died on the *Ben Hur* shoot. You said you were sure it had something to do with all this, didn't you?'

'Yes, but his family and friends won't speak to anyone. They've been paid well.'

'I've been looking for him online,' said Jude. 'There are a few reports and some stuff on internet gossip sites. They're a bit yucky.' He pulled a face. 'I don't understand what half the stuff on them means.'

'Hmm,' said Tony. 'I'm not sure you should be reading them.'

'Why? They can't harm me if I don't know what any of it means.'

Tony could not argue with that logic. 'Never mind. What have you heard on these sites?'

'There's one forum where they keep deleting one member because he, or she, keeps bringing up this death and saying George Cassius is a murderer. The owners of the forum were told off by some lawyers so they're a bit scared now. But if someone thinks George Cassius is a murderer, maybe he is.'

Tony was not sure he liked that idea, considering that Patty had just left to go to work with Cassius, but he did not say so to Jude. He told himself there would be others there working too. But did he really know that? 'Let's er . . . let's have a look at this actor, Jude. Are there any pictures of him online? I don't think I even know what he looks like.' It was not strictly true. He had seen some pictures of the man in the insurance files. He just wanted to draw Jude away from the George Cassius angle. But he also wished that Margaret and Terence would return quickly. He wanted to go to the studio and check on Patty. It had been stupid of him to let her go alone! On the other hand, she was a grown woman, and as far as they knew, the two killers were in custody.

Except neither of them had really believed that. Not deep down. Patty had been right when she said it felt like an anti-climax. Apart from Andy Paxton's previous relationship with the two men, nothing had pointed towards them killing Jason and Olivia too. It did not make sense. Plus, Peter Harris seemed like a nice, decent bloke, even if Vince Astwell was a bit of a shark. Tony realised that he, too, was being swayed by the quiet dignity of Harris's grandmother. She believed so much in her boy, and that conviction was contagious.

Jude put the actor's name, Simon Naughton, into the search engine. Tony got up off the edge of the bed and went to look over his shoulder. 'Click on images,' he suggested.

'Yeah, I know, Tony,' Jude tutted.

A page full of images came up on the screen, showing Simon Naughton on various locational shoots, or standing next to a more famous actor. He had been very well respected, judging by some of the comments below the pictures when they opened them. But nothing told Tony or Jude anything they needed to know. Naughton had never worked with Jason Carter, Andy Paxton or Olivia before. 'Try the next page, mate,' said Tony, doubting they would get much. Even by the bottom of the first page, the pictures had changed to those of men with either the same or a similar name to Simon Naughton. The man had not been famous enough to build up a huge following. Like Matt Archer, the film with George Cassius had been his big break.

Then they found it several pages in, on the obscure blog of a film fan. It was not a brilliant picture, but it was clear enough.

Simon Naughton and companion, Carla, attend the Sundance Film Festival.

Tony's head swam and all sorts of images and thoughts churned around his brain — of Simon Naughton's companion, and George Cassius being nice to Patty and politely asking her to work when he was seldom that nice to anyone. More importantly, Tony was reminded of George Cassius's inability to remember someone's name, and it just being dismissed as his usual rudeness. Only, if the picture was to be believed, he had recalled the name correctly.

'Jude,' he said urgently, 'we have to go out, mate.'

'Where?'

'To the studio. I can't leave you here,

so you'll have to come with me.' What would Patty think of him, taking Jude into possible danger? 'I wish your grandparents were back.'

'Is Mum in trouble, Tony?'

'I don't know. I might be being stupid.'

'I want to come if she's in trouble. We have to help her.'

'Yes, we do. And if we're wrong, we can have a good laugh about it later, hey?' He prayed he was wrong, because if anything happened to Patty, he did not know what he would do.

And if anything happened to Jude because Tony had put him in a dangerous situation, she might never forgive him.

20

Patty knew something was wrong the minute she entered the sound stage. There were no crew members going about their business, or other actors getting into costume. All she could see was the set, on which stood a sarcophagus. Several days before, there was more around the tomb, including the cross-section of a pyramid built out of MDF. Now there was only the tomb and it was under a spotlight, as if to draw her to that spot.

She shivered, realising that she was not entirely alone. There was a single camera rig trained on the sound stage. It was on wheels and had a seat behind it which moved and swung up through the air. It was mostly used for big action shots, not intimate scenes. Whoever was up there was lost in the shadows.

In reality, she had known it would come to this. That was why she was not convinced about Harris and Astwell being arrested. She knew she had one more scene to play, and she had fought against it with all her might.

How could she leave her precious son? How could she leave Tony, now that she had found him and learned to love him so deeply? Her breath caught in her throat. Would they think she had taken the decision to die? Perhaps the police would put it down to her grief over Jason's death. She could just turn and run away, yet something kept her rooted to the spot. It was not a wish for death. It was a wish for truth. If she was ever going to find out what happened, she knew she would have to play out this scene.

'George?' she said, looking up to the camera and making an educated guess. He had phoned her, after all.

'Hello, Patty,' he said.

He was so far away from her that she could have run. By the time he had brought the camera to the ground, she would be out of the door and off up to security.

'Why, George? Is this how you want to be remembered? As a killer?'

'Patty, it's not me. I swear it.' The camera moved suddenly, causing Patty to jump. She was about to run when the spotlight that lit up the tomb moved to the person sitting on the camera.

It was George Cassius, but he was bound with tie wraps. There was blood on his forehead and he looked deathly pale. Patty ran towards him, meaning to help him escape, but the camera swung into the air, beyond her reach, casting George in shadow again.

'You're to go and sit on the tomb,' he said.

'No, I'm not going to do that, George. I have a son.' Tears pricked Patty's eyes. If she ran away, Cassius might be dead before she reached the security room. She could not leave him to die alone, even if he was a horrible man who cared about no one but himself. 'I have people I love. I won't leave them.'

'Then get out, Patty, whilst you can.'

'No, I'm not leaving you either.'

'I don't deserve your pity,' said Cassius. 'I've done terrible things.'

'What are you saying? Are you saying that you did kill Jason and the others?' Patty frowned.

'No, not them. I killed Simon Naughton. I knew the set-up for the stunt wasn't secure. And he died because of it. It was manslaughter, even if it wasn't murder.' It sounded as if Cassius was reading from a script. There was no conviction in the words. He would never admit to such a thing if he were not under duress. But where was the pressure coming from? Patty cast her eyes around the studio, trying to make out another figure in the darkness.

'Who is doing this, George?'

'You're to go and sit on the tomb, Patty. That's all I'm allowed to say.'

'I'm not going to do that.' She remained rooted to the spot, even though every instinct told her to run. When she had acted out such scenes, in woman-in-peril dramas, she often wondered why the characters did not just run like hell to the nearest safe place. Now she understood why. She was too frightened to move in any direction, unsure if a wrong move would lead to her death anyway.

She guessed there was someone else in the studio, because someone had to have tied George up, but it was only then that she felt their real presence. Evil filled the air with a bitter aroma that made Patty want to gag.

'Go to the stage, Patty,' said George in a mechanical voice.

As if in a trance, Patty started to move forward, toward the gold tomb that was to have been Cleopatra's last resting place. Would it be hers? Her whole body trembled, and her mind whirled with images as she tried to work out how she was going to get out of this mess. And she would have to. She could not leave Jude and Tony. She thought about her parents too, and a sob caught in her throat at the thought of never seeing them again. Please God, she prayed, if you are there, let them know that I did not plan this. Let them know that I loved them with all my heart.

She reached the tomb and then turned to face the camera, almost as if she had been directed to do so. She could not touch the gold MDF box behind her. It was almost as if she feared a snake would jump out of it and bite her.

'I'm in the wrong costume,' she said, playing for time and willing the person who was tormenting her to come out of the shadows. 'Jeans and a T-shirt are hardly fitting attire for the Queen of Egypt.'

'It won't matter,' said a voice from the darkness. It was a woman, and the voice was familiar. 'No one will know what you were wearing when all this is over.'

'Who is that?' Patty squinted and searched the shadows for a darker shadow. 'Carmen?'

Carmen stepped forward into the light. She held something in her hand, which was still in the shadows, but Patty could not work out what it was. With a shudder she wondered if it was a snake in a basket. 'At least you remembered my name,' said Carmen. 'I always liked you for that. Even though it's not my real name. Is it George? He did remember, you see, but when a man is as vile and unthinking as he is, getting someone's name wrong is brushed off as part of his charm. Or lack of it. My real name is Carla.'

'Very well, Carla, if that's your real name. What is all this about?'

'It's about the man I loved!' Carla's voice rose, becoming shrill, unhinged. 'Simon Naughton was a brilliant actor, and my lover. And he . . . ' she gestured towards the gantry. 'He took him from me. George Cassius ruined my life, and now I'm going to ruin his.'

'Fair enough,' said Patty, swallowing hard. 'George Cassius is a swine. We all know that. But Jason . . . ' her voice broke a little. 'My ex-husband was not responsible for what Cassius did. Neither were Andy and Olivia. And you left my son without a father! Surely with losing Simon you understand how that loss hurt.'

'Olivia was a mistake. She remembered seeing me with blood on my clothes when it shouldn't have been there. Anyway, as long as one handmaiden died it didn't matter. The police turning up prevented the other girl's death. I made her jump so she'd drop the cup. She was nervy enough to make it happen. The others, Jason and Andy, were just collateral. I had a different plan to begin with and only got the idea to kill them off in the same way as their characters in the original film because of the coincidence with the initials. Sometimes the innocent have to suffer so that the guilty can be brought to justice.'

'No.' Patty shook her head vigorously. 'No, they don't. Carm — Carla — I'm so sorry for your loss, but Andy and

Olivia did nothing to you. This is not the way to bring Simon back.'

'I'm not bringing him back. I'm going to join him.'

Patty felt righteous indignation rising in her chest. She would not be taken from her son and the man she loved by a madwoman. 'Why don't you go and get on with that and leave the rest of us be? I've done nothing to you. And even George hasn't. It was just a tragic accident.'

'Oh yes, that's why Cassius paid off Simon's family and made them sign a confidentiality agreement. You don't know anything about it. You can't know how I've suffered. I thought you were a nice person, but actually you're just as fickle as the rest of them. You didn't even cry when your ex-husband died and it hasn't taken you long to find someone else.' Her tone was mocking and it made Patty's face flare with shame. She pushed the feeling aside angrily.

'That's not the way it is, Carla. Of

course I cried for Jason, but we hadn't loved each other for a long time. He was just a great friend to me. I felt his death more for my son than for myself. And I'm allowed to find love!' Saying it was a revelation to Patty. Since the divorce from Jason she had denied herself that right. It was her way of being loyal. When they had married, she had believed it was for life, and divorce did not change that for her, even if their love had died and he had moved on to other women. Whilst she would have done anything to stop Jason from dying, she was forced to admit that his death had given her the liberty to move on in a way she could not whilst he was still alive.

'You have to let go,' she said to Carla, though she was also telling herself the same thing. It was time to let go. If only she could live long enough to enjoy her freedom. 'If Simon was the wonderful man you say he was, he would not have wanted fathers taken from their children or young women taken from their families and the ones who loved them.

He knew the risks of being an actor. He signed up for it.'

'I loved him!'

'I know that, sweetheart. I understand and I know how much it hurts to lose him. But this . . . ' Patty spread her hands to encompass all the things that Carla had done. 'This is not the way to honour him.'

'You don't know anything. I will honour him and when I've finished no one will ever forget his name.'

'You think?' Patty had to keep talking. To keep playing for time. She sent up a silent prayer that Tony would realise she was in danger and come for her. Please, darling, she whispered inwardly. Please find me. 'Has it occurred to you that his family did not need to be paid to keep silent? They keep silent because they want to remember him in their own private way. If you finish what you started, it will be nothing but a nine-day wonder. Then next week some Z-list celebrity will get pregnant or adopt a baby from Korea and no one will care about what you've done in Simon's name. If he is mentioned again, it will only be in relation to death and heartache. Do you realise what sort of legacy you're creating for him? It's one where a madwoman murdered in his name.'

'I'm not mad!'

'No, no of course not,' Patty said in more conciliatory tones. 'No, you're hurting, I understand that.' She did not understand at all. Even though Carla had murdered Jason, whom Patty had cared for, she did not feel like killing the girl for it. Even less did she feel like going out and murdering a bunch of innocent people who had nothing to do with Jason's death. Carla was clearly certifiable and probably had been for some time. She wondered if Simon Naughton had known that. Was that why she clung to his memory so desperately? Because she had sensed him turning away from her? 'Tell me about him,' she said, playing for more time. 'Simon, I mean. How did you meet?'

'We met on the set of *Ben Hur*, of course.'

'Oh, I see. So you didn't know him before then?'

'I'd heard of him. It was me who suggested to George that he take Simon on.'

Patty had almost forgotten about George. She wanted to ask him if he was okay, but she did not want to draw too much attention to him in case it sent Carla on a rampage. 'You obviously admired Simon very much.'

'I'd been trying to meet him for ages. I saw him at the Sundance Film Festival. It was funny really,' said Carla, reminiscing. 'Because we weren't actually together, but there's a picture of us online that says, 'Simon Naughton and companion'. The blogger thought I was Simon's girlfriend even then.'

Patty wanted to scoff, because the relationship with Simon Naughton had obviously been very fleeting, if it had been a relationship at all. Then she remembered how little time she had really known

Tony before falling in love with him. She had not told him she loved him. She had been afraid to say it because she had known all along that she was moving towards this final scene. All the more reason she should have said it, she realised now, with the clock ticking and her chances of surviving this night being slim. 'Obviously you were meant to be together,' said Patty, then immediately regretted it when she saw the look on Carla's face. She had the look of an early Christian martyr, and that was very dangerous.

'You do understand,' said Carla, nodding. 'Then I'm very sorry this has to happen to you. I have to finish this now, don't you see?'

Yet she seemed to be waiting for something. Or someone. Of course! For the little drama Carla had created to play out, there was one more sacrifice to be made. Matt Archer was either on his way to the studio or Carla already had him somewhere. Patty guessed the former. But how on earth would a tiny girl like Carla overcome Matt? Somehow she had managed it with George, and though he was only average height, he was still a burly man. Maybe the same fear that bound Patty in one place would make Matt acquiesce.

'Yes, I see.' Patty glanced towards Carla's hand and suddenly the trance that had kept her rooted to the sound stage lifted. She wanted to live, to be with her son and the man she loved, and there was no way she was going down without a fight. Even if she died, they would know then that she had tried her hardest to stay with them.

Before Carla could move toward her, Patty dived from the stage with a resounding scream.

21

Tony drove through the studio gates, glancing in his rear view mirror as he did so. The security guard had told them that Patty had gone to sound stage nine.

'Are we being followed?' asked Jude.

'In a manner of speaking. In that someone is following us into the studio.'

The car behind continued to follow them to sound stage nine, pulling up behind them in the area where the trailers were parked.

'Stay there,' said Tony. 'Don't move from the car.' He handed Jude his phone. 'If there are any problems, dial the police straight away. Okay?'

'Yes, okay.'

Tony did not really want to get out of the car. He had never known such a feeling of being torn in two. He wanted to know if Patty was safe, but was afraid to take Jude into the studio in case there was danger. He did not want to leave Jude alone in case he was hurt. He wondered if this was how all fathers felt when caring for their loved ones. Had his own father felt as torn when Tony and his brother Will had fallen out over that girl? It must have been really hard for Harry to love both his sons and yet have them so against each other. Then for that not to be resolved before Will died . . .

Tony shook himself. By losing himself in the past he was putting off the inevitable — that moment when he would have to make the decision to leave Jude alone. But he vowed silently that he would never do that again. Just as soon as Patty was safe. 'Stay here, mate.'

'Yeah, you said that.'

'I know. I should have left you with the security guard.' Now why had he not thought of that at the gates? In fact, why had he not told the guard he suspected there was trouble? His head full of 'should have done's, Tony got out of the car.

At the same time, the driver of the car parked behind got out.

'Matt? What brings you here?'

'I had a message from Patty, saying she wanted to meet me here.'

Tony stopped and stared at Matt. Oh dear God! Had Patty made an assignation with Matt? He had no way of knowing if it was really George Cassius on the phone earlier. Immediately, Tony's mind went to Jude again. Whatever his personal feelings on the matter, he could not drag the child into such a scenario. It might damage Jude indefinitely. 'Did she? Was that when you phoned earlier?'

'No, I didn't phone,' said Matt. 'She sent me a text.'

'Right . . . ' Tony's brow furrowed. 'When was this?'

'About half an hour ago. I have to say I was surprised. I thought you two were pretty thick now.'

'But still you came?' Tony raised an eyebrow.

'I was curious, I guess. I also wanted to . . .'

Before Matt could say anymore, they heard a scream from inside the studio.

'Patty!' Tony headed for the door, closely followed by Matt. Whatever plans she had made with Matt, he could not leave her in danger. 'No.' Tony turned back to him briefly, walking backwards awkwardly because he was so desperate to get inside. 'Stay with Jude, will you? He's in the car. Oh, and ring the police.'

Matt hesitated and seemed about to argue. Then he said, 'Sure, okay.'

Tony turned back and kicked open the sound stage door, even though it was not locked. The sight that met his eyes was astounding. Patty and another woman were rolling around the floor, fighting each other. Patty seemed to be trying to snatch something from the woman's hand.

As Tony moved toward them, he saw that it was a syringe. His eyes briefly took in the stage with the sarcophagus and he began to understand part of what was going on. This was supposed to be Patty's death scene and the syringe had some sort of poison in it.

Without really thinking too much, Tony kicked at the woman's hand, and she dropped the syringe. Before she could snatch it again, he crushed it underfoot and lifted Patty off her. 'You're safe, darling, you're safe . . . ' he said.

She threw her arms around him, sobbing. 'I thought I wouldn't see you again,' she said. 'I thought I wouldn't be able to tell you that I loved you.'

All Tony's doubts about Matt disappeared. It had all been set up by the girl Carla, or Carmen, or whatever she called herself. 'I'm here my love.'

Carla lay sobbing on the floor, clutching her swollen hand. Before Tony could get Patty out of there, she had recovered and ran towards them, her hands stretched out like talons. Tony caught hold of her and wrapped her in a half Nelson. 'Go outside,' he said to Patty. 'Jude and Matt are waiting. I'll hold her.'

'I have to get George down,' said Patty.

'George?'

'He's up in the gantry.' Whilst Tony wrestled with Carla, who was spitting and screaming, Patty went to the camera and pressed the button to bring it down to the ground again. She managed to undo the tie wraps and set George free.

'Go on,' she said. 'I'll wait with Tony.' George did not need telling twice.

'Patty, darling, go outside,' said Tony. 'Jude is waiting and he's worried about you.'

'But I'm worried about you.'

'I think I can handle this one.'

'You don't seem to be doing very well at it.' Patty smiled.

Like many people who were insane, Carla had immense strength, and she was giving Tony a really hard time.

'Mum!' said a voice from the door. 'Mum, are you okay?'

Jude was standing at the opening and

it helped Patty to make up her mind. 'Go on,' said Tony. 'He needs to see you're alright.'

* * *

Patty ran out of the studio and hugged her son. 'I'm fine, darling. I'm fine.'

Jude clung to her tightly. 'I thought I'd lost you too,' he said, crying.

'No, baby. That won't happen, I promise.'

'The police are on their way,' said Matt.

'Hi, Matt,' said Patty, with a tired smile. 'What brought you here?'

'Apparently a text from you.'

'I didn't send a text.'

'No, I'm guessing that now. But at least I could take care of Jude while Tony did his big hero thing. Not that Jude would stay in the car.'

'Thank you,' said Patty, reaching out and taking Matt's hand. 'Thank you so much.'

'You're welcome. Come on, sit in the

car until the police get here.'

George Cassius was sitting in the back of Matt's car, breathing into a paper bag. Patty went to him. 'Are you alright, George?'

'No, I'm not alright. Do I look alright? Bloody madwoman, ruining my film. I'll make sure she's locked up for good.'

'Well, you certainly seem better to me,' Patty laughed.

'I told them someone had it in for me, but would they listen? No.'

Patty had to admit that George had a point. It had all been about him. She realised he would be even more insufferable in future, but she also had a premonition that he would not work again. The nineteen sixties film of *Cleopatra* had nearly sunk Twentieth Century Fox, and she guessed the events surrounding the remake would sink George Cassius. She would never work with him again, not even if he won ten Oscars.

'Where's Tony?' asked Jude, holding tightly to his mum's hand.

'He's holding on to Carla till the police get here, only . . . ' Patty stopped suddenly. Carla had been sure that it would be the end of everything. Had she just intended to kill George, Matt and Patty, then herself? No, she had said something else. Something about how it didn't matter what Patty wore because no one would know, and then about joining Simon. 'Tony!' she screamed, just as an explosion ripped through the sound studio, sending debris up into the night air.

She threw Jude to the ground until the shock had abated. She was about to get up and run into the devastated studio, but Matt stopped her. 'Wait!' he ordered.

He ran inside, and was gone for what seemed like an age. At the same time the police arrived, and they called the fire brigade.

Patty sat on the ground holding Jude close to her, gulping back sobs. She could not lose Tony. Not now.

It seemed like forever, but was probably only five minutes later that Matt came out, carrying a figure in his arms. 'Oh God . . . ' Patty sobbed, as Matt lowered Tony to the ground. She ran to him and fell to her knees, lifting him into her arms. 'Is he . . . ?' she looked up at Matt.

'He's fine, just unconscious,' said Matt.

'Carmen?'

Matt shook his head. 'She took the force of the blast.'

Patty wanted to be sorry, but could not be. Not over a woman who had taken three lives and would have taken three more given half the chance. 'Thank you for bringing him back to me,' she said to Matt.

'Well, I never stood a chance did I?' said Matt with a smile. 'He's a good guy. Look after him.'

'I will.' She brushed Tony's hair back from his face. 'Tony, darling. Can you hear me?'

He opened his eyes. 'Hello, beautiful,' he said. 'Was that explosion big enough for you?'

'Oh don't joke,' she sobbed. 'I

thought I'd lost you.' She cradled him in her arms, rocking him like a baby.

'I couldn't die. I hadn't told you how much I love you.'

'And I love you too,' she said.

'This is the bit where you're supposed to take my breath away with a kiss,' he said, repeating Antony's last words to Cleopatra.

'Don't you dare say such things, Tony Marcus. If you die I'll never speak to you again.'

22

Patty, Tony and Jude carried the rest of their things into the clock tower cottage in the Castle Village, then when everything was in place, all three slumped down onto the sofa.

'Home at last!' said Patty, sitting between the two men she loved most in the world. She put her arms around their shoulders. Her new wedding ring glinted in the light from the afternoon sunshine coming through the windows. 'I thought we'd never get here.'

'I want to go and look at my new room,' said Jude.

'Alright, darling,' said Patty. 'We'll have fish and chips for tea, yes?'

'Yum!'

Alone at last, Patty and Tony fell into each other's arms. 'You're not upset about not having a honeymoon, are you, darling?' she asked.

'Of course not. We can't leave Jude after all that's happened. We've got the next fifty years to have a honeymoon.'

'Only fifty years?'

'Sixty, seventy, eighty . . . forever.' He stroked her face. 'Are you happy?'

'Yes, I've never been happier.'

'Not wishing you'd married Matt?'

'Matt didn't love me and I didn't love him. I think he was starting to love Olivia, but she was taken from him.' Patty looked sad for a moment, remembering the lovely girl who could have been her friend if they had more time to know each other. 'In fact, he told me that when he got a text from me asking him to meet me, he was wondering how to let me down gently.'

'I knew that man had no taste.'

Patty laughed, her momentary sadness gone. 'Make up your mind. He's either your love rival, or he's wrong for not loving me. If I love him at all, it's because he saved the man I truly love.'

'I know. I made him my best man, didn't I?'

'And I've asked him to be godfather.'

'Godfather? Oh you mean if we have a baby?'

'No, darling,' she said, kissing him. 'Not if. When.' She patted her tummy.

'When? And you've carried all this stuff into the house? Patty, my love, you should have said. Are you alright, darling? Do you need anything? A cup of tea? Or a cushion for your back? We have to tell Jude. He'll want to know.'

'Hush,' she whispered, putting her finger to his lips. 'We'll tell him over the fish and chips. But for now just kiss me and take my breath away.'

THE END